THE TIME DISSOLVER

By
JERRY SOHL

I0616858

ARMCHAIR FICTION
PO Box 4369, Medford, Oregon 97501-0168

*For more information about Armchair Books and products, visit our
website at…*

www.armchairfiction.com

Or email us at…

armchairfiction@yahoo.com

WHAT TERRIBLE THING WAS HE MADE TO FORGET?

A man awakens with a clear memory of his date the night before. He rises to go on about his business as usual—finds he is in a room he has never seen before. He looks in the mirror…it is his face he sees all right—but aged! He went to sleep on May 15th of one year. He awoke the next day as expected—but eleven years later! The woman in the bed beside him awakens also—in terror at the sight of him. She too went to sleep on May 15th…

Neither one had ever seen the other before!

CAST OF CHARACTERS

WALTER SHERWOOD
A scientist who has lost his science. Where have eleven years gone? Will he be his own salvation or his own destroyer.

VIRGINIA SHERWOOD
A wife, but she woke in a strange hotel room, in a strange city, next to a strange man. She too, had lost eleven years.

DR. BOOEY
The good doctor was Walter's friend and mentor. Could he help him continue on the path to remembrance?

DR. ANDREW SCHLESSENGER
He was top dog at a big institute and Walter's boss. Why did he seem so strangely unwilling to help?

HAMPTON AND KITTY COX
These two were Walter's ray of light in a dark cave of lost memory and uncertain intentions.

GEORGIA SCHLESSENGER
A powerful lady with a lot of money. She seemed so desperate, yet she also seemed completely unwilling to talk about it.

OLIVER LANSING
Walter's lab assistant. Would he be able to help Walter and Virginia get their memories back—before it was too late?

CHAPTER ONE

MUFFLED SOUNDS OF traffic filled the room, ebbing and flowing around the two sleepers who, as if subconsciously sensing that the rest of the world was awake and busy and that they should be up and doing, too, stirred in sleep. The girl's lips moved soundlessly as she lay on her back, a signal to move again, which she did, bringing her knees up under the covers as she turned on her side facing the windows. She sighed contentedly when the maneuver was completed. The man, unmoving during this, took his turn, shifting from a position on one side to the other, facing her now, bunching the sheet and blanket beneath an elbow, leaving no covering for his bare back side.

It was the hour when sleep is lightest, when sleep is sweetest, and Walter Evan Sherwood, who, had thus far resisted the call of traffic and sounds of life's reawakening, finally grudgingly assented to an experimental look-see at the prospect of this day, opening his eyes to mere slits, studying the girl's black hair and the smooth expanse of flesh beneath it, deciding at once that if this was true this day would lead all the rest. He lay there, unwilling to shatter the illusion of black hair on pillow, the fine line of back that disappeared beneath the covers thinking, *it's so real I feel as if I could reach out and touch it oh the fantasies of this end of sleep there she is no doubt manifestation of my repressed desires.*

He looked languishingly but the image did not shimmer or blur or blend into another as he expected it would; instead the hair became more life-like, the flesh more tantalizingly real. Now his eyes were no longer narrowed, his heart no longer the slow, steady heart of sleep, his breathing not that of a sleeping man as he looked away from the shining black hair and neck and shoulders and saw that the room was strange to him. He looked back at the girl as she stirred again, turning to him, a movement of arm dislodging the covers to expose a well-rounded shoulder and breast, eyes still closed in sleep, her full lips petulant, as if she were waiting to be kissed. She was pretty and he let it go at that, forcing his eyes back to the room itself, the pebbly white ceiling, gray walls, blinded windows, desk, drawer, bureau.

Sherwood slipped quietly from the bed, stood looking down at the sleeping girl, decided she was in her late twenties, then with a shock discovered he was naked, which was not as much of a shock as the discovery that his pajamas were in a heap at his feet—not his pajamas, but a man's pajamas. He was tempted to put them on, then saw a man's clothes on a nearby chair: blue shorts, white undershirt, gray herringbone trousers, white shirt, maroon tie, suit-coat to match the pants, maroon socks and black shoes. He had no recollection of owning these particular clothes, did not want to put them on, but knew he could not continue to stand there as he was.

Where did I go last night? he asked himself as he put on the clothes. *How did I end up here? I went to sleep after being out with Marion didn't I? Then how did I get here? I don't even know this girl, I never saw her before in my life but she's prettier than Marion.*

The clothes fitted perfectly, but then he knew somehow they would, and he marveled at the impossibility of it. He turned to look at the girl again, was startled to find her sitting up, her round and frightened blue eyes meeting his, the bedclothes drawn up in two small fists beneath her chin, exposing the curve of both shoulders.

My God, he thought, from the looks of her I don't belong here. Could I have lost my way thinking this is my place, coming in and getting in bed with her? No, but I can't stay here. I don't want to stay here. Pretty soon she'll start screaming and then there'll be trouble and I don't even know where the door is.

He found the door in a small alcove, stepped quietly out into bright sun, squinted and tried to orient himself. He'd never been here before. He stood on a red cement stoop with wrought iron railings; there were three steps to the white crushed stone of a driving area. To his right along the drive were other doors with identical stoops and railings, to his left it was no different. His view ahead was obstructed by a larger white frame building.

Sherwood stepped to the drive, walked along it to the side of the larger building where it curved to a street, a wide street, feeling the whole experience was merely an extension of a dream. He squinted. Something was wrong with his eyes. The street was there but the traffic was blurry and lacked detail. He walked to the street. It looked like Colorado Boulevard, but where on Colorado was he? He turned to see where he had come from. The large white structure had plate glass windows facing the street and a large neon sign above it proclaimed it CORONADO MOTEL. So I took her to a motel. Or did she take me?

CHAPTER TWO

HE STARTED BRISKLY down the street, his step that of a confident man, looking for landmarks but finding none immediately, his eyes refusing to focus on distant things, and his step slowed as he thought *what did she feed me what did we drink I never had a hangover like this before*, and he finally came to a full stop at a corner when his mind, obsessed with the strangeness, no longer gave directions to his feet.

Look, he told himself, *yesterday was a fine day where did it go wrong? I'd been out of the army a week and I sat in the contour chair on the patio stewing most of the day away. Let's begin with that.*

There was the recollection of his mother watching him through the kitchen window. She was worried about him, he knew that, worried about what the army had done to him, and she had craftily tried to draw him out, but he didn't feel like talking. He could have said yes, Dad's death did things to me, no, I'm not exhibiting symptoms of what he had it's just that getting out of the army is quite a jolt, that's all, but he didn't say anything and he knew her worry only deepened because of it. The truth was he wanted to think about his father and all the things he'd seen and done, and to weigh the direction he'd decided to go.

But that wasn't all. There was Marion, the date with her, and he remembered how she came out of the house, a long-legged, trim figure in a summery cinnamon dress, and hew he groaned when he saw the high heels because he wasn't dressed where those heels wanted to go.

They hadn't gone anywhere, except down Colorado, south on Glendale to Sunset and out to Santa Monica where they parked by the beach and he brooded and she had politely asked him what was wrong. He told her a little about it, about how it had been from the time of induction in October, 1942, until plunk went the bomb and the olive-drab life was over abruptly in May, 1946, and how it felt to come home, how it was like being naked on the street out of uniform. But he didn't tell her about how close he'd been to his father even after his father's sickness, didn't tell her how it felt to have him die like that in a sanitarium while he was in the army, how it was in the Medics when he saw men break down just as his father had done and how each cry and scream reminded him of it. He couldn't have told her about that. He couldn't even discuss it with his mother.

Then I went home, didn't I? I put the convertible in the garage on Colorado and walked up to the house on Dahlia Drive because I wanted to stretch my muscles and think because I ought to do something with myself at twenty-five, and I went up to my room and lay there looking out at the moonlight and the palms. I thought about the way my father used to look at me sometimes, that look of agony and mute plea for help I could never give, and I thought how I'd seen that same look on faces I'd seen in the army, and I remember I— what? Did I fall asleep just then? Why is it so hazy?

He shook his head as if to clear it, looked around at the buildings shimmering in the sunlight. Remembering yesterday wasn't helping today. Deciding to go down Colorado until he came to an area he knew, he struck off across the street and walked until he came to a familiar drive-in. This point was three blocks from where he always turned off Colorado on Dahlia Drive. With the drive-in as an anchor, he hurried over the intervening blocks, conscious that the surroundings had somehow changed but trying not to think about it, eventually coming to the garage where he had put his convertible for the night. He hesitated on the sidewalk, but not sure he should enter the garage because it too seemed somehow different. What was wrong with everything?

It was then he saw himself in the garage window and jerked back in surprise.

Can that be me?

He forced himself to stand quietly while he inspected his image. The man who stared back at him was heavier than he, but he was obviously Walter Evan Sherwood, nonetheless, a hatless man with wide eyes, heavy brows, thick hair, wearing a neat suit that didn't belong to him, but the total man was different from the Walter Evan Sherwood he was fused to seeing in mirrors. What was the difference? Trick window? He moved about; there was no distortion. Where was the change? He moved closer, studied his reflection carefully. And suddenly he knew.

He was older.

But I could not have changed like that overnight, he protested. No one could. But his argument did not erase what he saw before him.

Deeply troubled and dismayed, Sherwood turned from the window. He walked less briskly now, still tried unsuccessfully to make his eyes pierce the haze and blur of distance, examined the traffic with new interest, finding the cars different, too—newer, shinier and strange.

He felt a little reassured when he crossed Colorado and started up Dahlia Drive because things hadn't changed much here. The same bright houses, the same well-kept green lawns and trees and palms.

At length he reached the house, stood staring at it in disbelief because it had changed so. The gravel driveway they had always wanted to pave was a wide slab of cement now, the house was a maroon with white trim instead of—what was it before? Pastel green with white trim? The rose bushes were gone from the front yard, the window boxes were gone too, and the roof was a new mottled gray. These were not overnight changes, he told himself, and he did not want to think how many nights and days they represented.

He went up the walk, bypassed the front door, let himself through the white gate, walked along the side of the house, noticing the profusion of growing things, the clipped and clean and watered and thriving plants and flowers and shrubs, eventually emerging to the back yard. The contour chair was not on the patio. Now what the hell had she done with the contour chair? That was his; he had made it a special way so it could be taken apart in the middle and collapsed so it could be carried in a car trunk. And it should have been there.

Sherwood was on the point of angrily entering the house to demand an accounting when he heard a baby cry inside. A short, whimpering cry. He could not imagine whom it could be, mounted the steps slowly, reached for the porch doorknob, then drew his hand away. Things were too changed for casual entry.

A woman he had never seen before padded out on the porch in slippers and a faded housecoat. She was about thirty and probably had been a pretty girl ten years before. Now her face was dull and puffy, there were folds of skin beneath her chin, and she looked as if she didn't care for her hair any more.

"Yes?" she inquired coldly through the screen door, making no move to open it.

"Is—is Mrs. Sherwood at home?" he asked, feeling ridiculous for asking it and wanting to shout what the hell are you doing in my house.

"Mrs. Who?"

"Mrs. Sherwood, damn it," he said, tired of the changes, angry over the missing contour chair, put out with the stranger before him. After a moment he said, "She's my mother."

"Your mother?" She ogled him, backed away a little from the door, saying, "I don't know any Mrs. Sherwood. You sure you got the right address?"

"I—I used to live here," he stammered. "I've been away."

She eyed him suspiciously, said nothing.

Suddenly he remembered something. "Do the Thompsons still live next door?"

"A Mrs. Thompson does," the woman said. "You better go see her."

"Thanks," he said emptily. He went down the steps, crossed the yard as he had done thousands of times. There was little change next door. The same bird bath, the same silver ball on its pedestal, the round flowerbed in the middle of the yard. This was familiar. That same flowerbed used to make old man Thompson mad. He'd get fed up with having to cut around it with the mower, tried to get his wife to abandon it, but she never would.

He rang the Thompson back door bell.

The moment Mrs. Thompson saw him she said, "Walter Sherwood!" and opened the door for him. "I was watching you through the window and I thought it was you. Come in, come in!"

Cheered by the greeting, Sherwood managed a smile, stepped through the door.

"Sit down, sit down," she said, pulling out a chair for him. "I'll warm up some coffee." She turned on the heater beneath the percolator, saying, "My, it's good to see you." She paused. "Aren't you going to sit down?"

"Yes. Thank you." He'd just had a good look at her and it startled him. Now he sat and looked at her again. Mrs. Thompson had grown old. Her hair, once only shot through with silver, now was completely white, and her bright red cheeks, once the mark of Mrs. Thompson, had paled and all but collapsed, and the eyes—they had always protruded a bit—were yellowed and veined, and he thought for the thousandth time *my God what has happened to everything and everybody?*

"You haven't changed much, Walter," she said, taking the chair opposite him. She smiled ruefully and said, "You ought to see Jimmy. He's blossomed out. Can't get enough to eat, he says." She laughed a little.

Jimmy had been a boyhood friend; he and Sherwood had grown up together. Out of politeness he asked, "Where is Jimmy?"

"Work. He'll be home at five-thirty. Can you stay?"

"No, I'm afraid not."

"Oh, that's too bad. Jimmy'll be heart-broken he missed you."

"Mrs. Thompson," he said, digging right in, "do you recall the last time we saw each other? I don't seem to remember."

"Saw each other?" She frowned in recollection. "Why, I just don't know. Let me see, wasn't it when the house...no." She shook her head. "The real estate people handled that, didn't they? Can't you remember?"

"No."

Her study deepened. "I don't seem to either. And it's not like me to forget a thing like that, Walter. Mmm." Her eyes closed in intense concentration. Suddenly they blinked open and she said, "I know. It was the funeral."

Sherwood swallowed hard and said in a strangled voice, "The funeral?"

She nodded, lips pressed together in affirmation. "Yes, I'm sure of it now. It was the funeral."

Sherwood dropped his hands to the table, pressed the palms down hard on tablecloth, wet his lips and said in a soft voice, "Whose funeral, Mrs. Thompson?"

She gave him a startled glance. "Whose?"

"Yes."

"Why, your mother's, of course." She lowered her eyes. "We felt so bad about it, coming so soon after your father's." Then her eyes came up with a puzzled look. "Of course you remember that, don't you?"

Sherwood stared at the backs of his hands on the table, his mind trying to accept the fact of his mother's death, feeling suddenly empty, so alive yesterday, so dead today, except that his today was different from Mrs. Thompson's because hers was so far removed from his yesterdays and he had no recollection of tee passage of time to dull the feeling of personal loss.

"When did she die?"

"When? Why, the year after you got out of the army. She was left all alone, poor dear, while you went off to school. But I would think you would remember a thing like that."

"I don't remember it at all."

Mrs. Thompson sucked in her breath. Then she said, "What's happened to you?"

"I don't know, Mrs. Thompson."

The coffee was boiling but she made no move toward the stove. She stared at him with wide eyes instead. She said, "Your father—" and then stopped.

He looked up. "It started like this with my father, is that what you were going to say?"

"Well, I—" Her hand went to her throat and in looking away she suddenly spied the coffeepot and turned off the heater. "The coffee's done."

"What year is this?"

"What year?" Mrs. Thompson's face had lost a great deal of its color. If her bands had not been occupied with the coffeepot they would have shaken. Her voice was shrill when she said, "Nineteen fifty-seven."

"Fifty-seven!"

She drew back from pouring the coffee. "Are you sure you're all right, Walter? Isn't there someone I could call?"

"What month is this?"

"July." The voice quivered.

"Day?"

"The fifteenth."

He snorted, fixed her with an unwinking gaze and said, "Do you know what day this is?"

"Whatever do you mean, Walter?" She still stood in the middle of the kitchen floor with the coffeepot, her eyes large and frightened.

"It's the day after my birthday, Mrs. Thompson. On your yesterday I was thirty-seven, but I don't remember anything after May fifteenth, nineteen forty-six, because that's yesterday to me."

"Oh!" Mrs. Thompson looked ready to run from the room with the coffeepot.

"You were going to pour coffee," he reminded her.

"Yes, yes." She hurriedly filled the cups and then put the percolator back on the stove.

"You said I went to school," he prompted, stirring the coffee.

"Yes." She was making a valiant effort for control. "You went to Illinois Midwest."

"I thought I'd planned to go to UCLA."

"No, you went to Illinois Midwest." She did not touch her coffee but kept her eyes steadily on his.

"When did I graduate?"

She said miserably, "I don't know, Walter."

"You're frightened."

"Please tell me who to call."

"You think I'm going—you think I've gone off my rocker, don't you?"

"You need help, Walter." She chanced a look at the kitchen clock.

Sherwood didn't know what the look meant, but he could not risk staying here. She thought he was crazy, there was no doubt of that, and as a result her usefulness to him was ended. There was someone else who could help him, a girl with shiny black hair, the girl he had left at the motel, if she was still there. She had looked at him much the way Mrs. Thompson was, a frightened look—but when the girl had looked at him was it fear caused by his lack of recognition of her or fear caused by her lack of recognition of him?

"I must be going," he said, getting up from the table. Mrs. Thompson nodded, staring, making no move toward amenities.

"The coffee was strong but good." He smiled down at her woebegone face. "Tell Jimmy hello."

Her eyes followed him out to the back porch, lost him when he turned from the door.

I was a fool to come up here, to run for my mother, he thought as he walked briskly down the street. I should have questioned the girl instead of running out on her the way I did. She could have told me what happened, where I found her, what we were doing ill the motel, where I got these clothes.

He noticed again that he could not see any great distance and he wondered if he were living in a shell beyond which things ceased to exist, to be created before him, to be destroyed behind him, depending upon which direction he was going, but then he thought that's not so fantastic if I can change from twenty-five to thirty-seven overnight anything is possible.

Then the thought he'd been holding in the back of his mind and had not dared think about came crashing home: *maybe this is the beginning, the beginning of what my father had, that forgetfulness, that dazed condition between violences I came to know so well in him, all of it so long ago, and all of it preceding the horrible things* that came later. The thought made his flesh crawl.

Going crazy!

No. He made himself repeat the word over and over until he felt some measure of calm. I can still think logically. Or is that what they all think just before... *No! What is this really now? I'm not insane, only forgetful, forgetful of— eleven years. A long time to forget, and to forget so completely.*

Amnesia?

I've got to talk to that girl!

CHAPTER THREE

SHERWOOD'S STEPS, so brisk when he left Mrs. Thompson's, slowed as he neared the Coronado Motel, and stopped altogether when he reached the drive he had walked down more than an hour before. He stood on the driveway in the shade of the office, an ambivalent man, suddenly wishing he had a cigarette. For the first time since he left the motel he searched pockets of the coat and trousers. They were empty.

He wanted to see the girl, talk to her, yet was held back by what he did not know of her, or himself. If he went in and revealed his inability to recall the events that led to their sharing the motel and bed, it might complicate rather than simplify things. But was there any choice? If he left there with only the clothes on his back and nothing in his pockets, what would he do? Wherever he went, whatever he did, he'd have to explain why he had no money, and who would believe his story? He'd no doubt end up in a psychiatric ward, and he thought *maybe that's where I'll end up anyway after I start talking to the girl, or maybe I ought to bypass her and just give myself up and have done with it.*

As he mused, he ran a finger along his jaw, feeling the stubble there. At the same time he identified the vague ache in his stomach as that of hunger. Suddenly he knew there was no alternative; he'd have to go in.

He crunched up the driveway, walked up the steps and opened the screen door. The inside door was locked. He was baffled again, looked around to make sure he had the right place, saw the button and pushed it, hearing the pleasant chime inside. No one came.

Sherwood moved off the steps, pondering his next move, wondering if the girl had gone back to sleep (no, she wouldn't have done that), if she just refused to answer the door (that was more likely), or if she had gone out (possible).

"What's the matter, Mr. Fisher, forget your key?"

Sherwood turned to look into the amused eyes of a tall, lanky man in a sports shirt and Levis coming up the drive.

"I'm not—" Sherwood started to say he wasn't a man named Fisher, but thought the better of it. For some reason he must have given this man that name; considering the girl inside, he could understand why.

"I'm not sure what I did with it," he said instead.

The man was old, and his crewcut seemed at first incongruous with the deeply etched face, but he did have bounce, stepping lightly to the door and inserting a key.

"Be surprised how many folks forget their keys," the motel man said. "Happens all the time. Always forgetting something, they are. Be surprised, too, how many things they leave behind." He turned and spat a blob of yellow over the iron railing. "Always getting a telegram or a special delivery letter saying 'Send me this' or 'Send me that' and telling me what cottage they left it in." He chuckled. "Once they even left a baby, but they knew I couldn't send that. Came back for it awful quick. But they did leave a dog once. Still got it, too." And as Sherwood made a move to go inside, the man went on, "Everything all right, Mr. Fisher?"

"Everything's just fine," Sherwood said with a straight face.

"Well, you just let me know if it isn't. Have to keep you folks happy, you know, or business will go right by the door." He chuckled again. "Or maybe I should say 'doors,' eh?" He laughed now. Sherwood guessed it was his standard joke. "Be seeing you, Mr. Fisher."

Sherwood closed the door softly behind him. The inside was dim and it took a moment for his eyes to get used to it, but even before they did he knew she wasn't there. There was no sound, no light, no sense of occupancy.

He walked into the combination living room-bedroom, saw that the bed had been made, but of the girl there was no sign. He told himself ruefully she didn't live there, so there was no sense in her leaving anything, clearing out after it was all over, maybe wanting to be sure to be gone by the time he got back. But her face kept flashing in his mind like" a neon sign.

He moved about the room, saw the folded pajamas on the chair. Had she done that? Or was it the cleaning woman? He opened the paneled doors of a storage compartment, saw a man's suit, sports coat and trousers hanging there, two pairs of shoes and a pair of slippers on the floor. Two suitcases were there, too; they bore the initials MDF in gold. He opened them; they were empty. He went to the bureau, opened the drawers, found shirts, socks, underwear and ties, then examined the objects on top. Billfold, road map of California, a book of Traveler's Checks, glasses in a case, a soiled handkerchief, a ring of keys, comb, lighter and a pack of cigarettes.

Sherwood took a cigarette, lighted it, trying not to feel like a thief. He drew a gratifying breath, then turned to the other items. The glasses—would they fit him? He withdrew them from the leather case. Horn rimmed. They did not look to be of great magnification. He was about to put them on when he had a thought. He went to the bathroom, turned on the lights and looked at his face in the mirror. On the bridge of his nose he saw two faint marks. Only then did he put the glasses on. They fitted perfectly and brought his eyes more clearly in focus.

So I wear glasses, he thought, returning to the living room. *That is, if I am the man to whom all this belongs, and I'm beginning to doubt I'm anybody else. I should have worn the damn things when I went out before. Maybe I'd have seen things better.*

Now Sherwood picked up the billfold, withdrew an Illinois driver's license. He stared in amazement at the name. Morley Don Fisher. Address: 1213 Summit Ave. City: Wester. County: Macon. Sex: Male. Height: 6' 1". Weight: 185 pounds. Date of birth: July 14, 1920. Color hair: Black. Color eyes: Blue. The license was due to expire Jan. 10, 1958. The description, except for the name, fitted him perfectly.

He took out the rest of the papers. Social Security card for Morley Don Fisher. Number 320-01-7129. He didn't remember his number, but he doubted it was this one. Honorable discharge facsimile in laminated plastic case. Mr. Fisher again, serial number 36741234, same physical description. The tour of duty even covered much of the same area Sherwood had been in, but his own serial number had been 35552952. Car license certificate for Mr. Fisher. He drove a 1956 Chevrolet. He wondered if it was in the garage adjoining the motel.

It was.

He returned from the garage to sit on the bed and give serious consideration to the problem. He had changed his identity for a reason. What reason? Criminal? His thoughts turned inward to probe the degree of crime he would be capable of. Then he thought of the honorable discharge. *I never served in the army under that name and I could never get the army to help me cover up my identity so this must be bigger than that. The question is, how big? Now there are two problems: First, how and why did I lose my memory, and second, how and why did I lose my identity as Walter Evan Sherwood? Plus the business about the girl, I mustn't forget that.*

He chewed his lower lip in frustration, the magnitude of these questions and the total absence of even the beginning of an answer to any of them becoming apparent for the first time. As his mind revolved about the dilemma, he once more became conscious of his hunger. He decided he would make better progress fortified with a good meal, but first there was a little question of being able to pay for it.

The billfold on the bureau yielded nothing. There, was no change either, which was strange. He thought of the girl again and decided he must have been trustful of her the night before, maybe a little too trustful. Then Sherwood picked up the Traveler's Checks, counted eight one hundred-dollar checks still attached. There would be no problem with the signature. It was exactly as he would sign Morley Don Fisher, a plain, exact, slanting bit of penmanship.

He put the checkbook in his pocket, left the motel, careful to see that one of the keys fitted the lock, and made his way down Colorado, entering the first place he came to, a clean, airy establishment that specialized in milk shakes and grilled hamburgers.

As he sat eating the first meal he could remember in eleven years, he became conscious of the stare of the man who sat on the stool next to his. At any other time he would have ignored the attention, for Los Angeles seemed to breed a certain species of people who spend their lives looking into other people's faces for a message, but under the circumstances Sherwood couldn't be sure what the man was reading into his.

Believing it best to meet such a challenge openly and boldly, Sherwood turned his head to the other, only to see the man turn away to his own meal. The stranger was a substantial man with graying hair, puffy cheeks and a receding chin who chewed his food as if he had no teeth. He was dressed in a crumpled bright Slimmer suit; his black shirt was open at the collar, exposing a wrinkled neck.

When Sherwood started to eat again, he felt the man's eyes on his cheek. He turned to him once more, quickly this time. The stranger, caught staring, leaned back, blew out his cheeks a little, and blinked his eyes.

"Pardon me," the man said in a thin, fiat voice.

"Why?" Sherwood asked.

"I guess I mistook you for somebody else."

"Who did you think I was?" He had been right about the man; he had no teeth. Sherwood wondered how he managed to cat his French fries and hamburger.

"You ever work at Paramount?"

"Not that I recall."

"You look like a guy I used to know over there."

"What was his name?"

"Gil Wetson. You sure you ain't him?"

"I'd know my own name, wouldn't I?"

"Sure, sure." The man took another chunk of the hamburger by putting it in his mouth, clamping his gums down on it, and tearing off what remained outside. He chewed it ruminatively, eyeing Sherwood all the while. "Sure is amazing," he said when he had followed his food with a little of the milk shake. "You and Gil'd pass as brothers, you know that?"

"I pity him."

"Oh, he's a nice guy, Gil is. But I ain't seen him for years. Wonder whatever happened to him."

"I wouldn't know."

They ate in silence for a few minutes, then the man said, "My name's Allerby, Hank Allerby."

And, Sherwood said to himself, it's a reliable device to get my name. He said, "What would you say if I told you my name is Walter Sherwood?"

"What should I say? 'Pleased to meet you'?"

"But it isn't Walter Sherwood."

"No?" Allerby looked at him skeptically.

"At least not at the moment it isn't. It's Morley Don Fisher."

"Is that so?"

Sherwood nodded. "Does the name mean anything to you?"

"No."

"Your name doesn't mean anything to me either."

"Sorry to hear that." Allerby sounded genuinely disappointed. Then he brightened, dipped a hand into a coat pocket. "Say, what you doing this aft?"

"This afternoon?"

"Yeah. Look." He showed Sherwood two tickets. "The reason I asked if you was Gil is I got passes to the game. You want to go?"

"Even if I'm not Gil?"

"Sure."

"What game is it?"

"What game? Why, the Angels—Los Angeles—of course." He withdrew the tickets. He eyed Sherwood suspiciously. "Maybe you ain't familiar with the teams we got out here."

"Well," Sherwood said, lacking anything better to say, "if it were the Cincinnati Reds now—"

"Reds!" Allerby glared. "You mean Redlegs, don't you?"

"Redlegs?"

"Where you been? Just where are you from, Mr. Fisher?"

"Why?"

"You don't sound like you keep up with baseball."

"Haven't followed it for about ten years."

"Well, no wonder, then."

Sherwood drank the last of his milk shake. "You mentioned this Gil Wetson."

"You know anything about him?"

"Suppose he were my brother?"

"Now we're getting someplace."

"And suppose he told me he woke up one morning and couldn't remember anything that happened during the past eleven years?"

Allerby smiled knowingly. "Not Gil. He wouldn't do a thing like that."

"Just suppose it happened, though. You look like an intelligent man, Mr. Allerby. What would you advise me to tell him?"

Allerby pursed his lips. "Gosh, I don't know. Maybe see a head-shrinker, I guess."

"Head shrinker?"

"Nut doctor. Say, nothing like that happened to Oil, did it?"

"Could be, Mr. Allerby. People lose their memories every day."

Allerby scowled into his food. "I sure hope nothing like that happened to him. Say, you sure you ain't Oil's brother?"

"No," Sherwood said, getting up. He left the man in the bright summer suit staring after him.

He had difficulty with the Traveler's Checks, but the girl at the cash register summoned the proprietor who cashed it for him. Then he went outside to Colorado Boulevard feeling much refreshed. He walked slowly along it, marveling at the changes, the new cars, and wondered whatever did happen to Gil Wetson, thinking I hope I don't turn out to be Mr. Allerby's old friend but anything seems possible. He noticed that his glasses helped him see distant scenes; the haze was still there, but at least he could define the objects he saw.

As he strolled along he let his mind wander to yesterday—the yesterday of his memory—and was surprised at the clarity of recall. He had picked up Marian at seven-thirty at her home, and he remembered every detail of her dress and how she looked, what they had done, his sullen mood, how long they had talked by the ocean and how it had somehow soothed him to do so. And then he had gone home, sick of indecision, to ponder what he must do with his life. The Walter Sherwood of that yesterday seemed strangely immature to him now.

I did something with my life, all right, he told himself wryly, and I don't even know what it is. I don't know whether to be happy or sad, to run in fear of my life or relax and enjoy myself in my new identity. I have eight hundred dollars, a car and clothes. I could have a real fling on that. Or maybe I should buy an island—it would have to be a small one for eight hundred dollars—and settle down there and try to figure this out.

The little talk with Mr. Allerby, pointless as it had been in most respects, had taught him one thing: He didn't know how things had changed in the past ten years. A little in significant thing like the Cincinnati Red*legs* *(Why in the world did I ever mention them? I never even followed them back in 1946.)* was a prime example. Now why had they changed the name? And then a thought struck him: *I don't even know who is President.*

It was early afternoon and Sherwood, seeking a remedy for the vacant decade of his mind, went to the nearest library to find it. He had the place to himself, except for the gimlet-eyed librarian who looked as if she expected him to slip a volume or two beneath his shirt any minute. *Why,* he mused, *am I getting all these stares from people? Or am I just self-conscious?*

"Can I help you?" the librarian said at last, coming over to the newspaper rack where he had been reading the headlines, some of which had no meaning for him. She was a thin creature with hair in a bun on the back of her neck, and wore thick glasses that gave her eyes that intense look. He yearned to tell her she ought to play a librarian's part in the movies.

"You might be able to help at that." Sherwood looked sourly at the papers. "It appears eleven years are missing."

"I beg your pardon."

"Do you have a file of Los Angeles papers from May sixteenth, nineteen forty-six, to date?"

"I'm afraid not," she said. "We keep them only a month. They are on microfilm at the downtown library, however."

"I see."

"You were looking for a certain news story? Perhaps the New York Times Index would help."

"I'm just trying to catch up on all the news for the past eleven years." She gave him such an uncomprehending look he hastened to add, "You'll get the picture better if you think of me as a man just freed after being in solitary confinement for eleven years."

She continued to ogle him, now with an overtone of repulsion, then came to a rapid decision. Marching to a shelf of reference books, she brought back a standard-size brown volume. "This is the current *World Almanac*," she said. "It has a chronology." She opened it, put it on the arm of the leather chair he was sitting in, pointed to a paragraph. "Nineteen forty-six begins right here. It takes you right up to late last year."

"Thank you."

"Not at all." She whisked herself away, the soul of efficiency.

Sherwood scanned the paragraphs. They presented in digestible brevity the memorial dates of the years. The first event of note after May 15 was a fire in the La Salle Hotel in Chicago on June 5, in which sixty-one persons were killed. He read on down the column, taking some satisfaction in the war criminals trial in which twenty-two Nazis were found guilty, reading of the coal mine strike, the resultant Taft-Hartley Act the next year, the assassination of Ghandi, the death of Benes and Masaryk, and the drama of the Berlin Airlift of 1948. The world had been a busy place, full of tensions and conflicts and charges and recriminations and he had had an unremembered part of it, though of course on a much smaller scale.

Sherwood chuckled when he read the account of the election of Truman, went on through the hanging of Japanese war criminals, the conflict in Israel, the exploding of an atom bomb in Russia. And then he was astonished to read of still another war, this time in Korea, coming so soon after the end of the war in Europe and the Pacific. Then there was an era in which everybody in the U.S. was worried about people in high places being communists, but it was two Puerto Ricans who tried to shoot their way in to kill the President. He found the recorded history almost unbelievable, as if someone had sat down and written the most fantastic things he could think of, the most frightening being the hydrogen bomb.

He read on through the election of Eisenhower, his reelection, the Suez Canal incident, and finally closed the book and leaned back in the leather chair and thought *we didn't really do much did we, fighting that war, because there is still discontent and uneasiness and violence and rioting.* But there were signs things were working out better. The United Nations, for one thing, and the change in Russia's attitude since the death of Stalin. Maybe there was reason to hope after all.

Sherwood glanced idly at the headlines of the newspapers in the rack, headlines that would be tomorrow's history, turning his head sidewise to read them One caught his eye and he leaned forward to see it better. It was a small story in the *New York Times* dated several days ago, and the headline said:

AMNESIA VICTIM STILL UNIDENTIFIED

Picking out the details, Sherwood read that a well-dressed girl had wandered into a precinct station in New York and said she couldn't remember her name or anything about herself. She was taken to Bellevue where she remained while doctors sought to determine the cause of her amnesia, while police tried to find out who she was.

The paragraph that interested Sherwood most was this one:

Dr. Harold Aspinall said late Tuesday the girl had suffered a blow on the right temple, which could account for her amnesia, though he explained the injury was hardly detectable. He also said it was not unusual for weeks or even months to pass before a patient recovered his memory in such cases.

Now Sherwood leaned back to consider this information. He had almost forgotten his affliction, accepting it as a thing irrevocable and willing to go on from there, reconstructing the pattern of his past by digging into it. Now he saw there was a possible shorter route, a direct line to the hidden past, a key that would unlock the remembrances he knew must still be there.

He reached up both hands, started pressing areas on his skull. An injury, that was it. A blow—what did the story say? Right temple? He pressed the right temple, then the left, ran exploring fingers over the remainder of his cranium seeking the injured spot. The girl could have done it. That would account for the look she gave him, the apprehension in her eyes, for she was wondering what her handiwork had wrought.

But there was no injured area he could find. But then he remembered the story said it was hardly detectable, so he pushed his fingers hard against his scalp, probing viciously for the sore spot that might be there.

He was so intent on his investigation he did not hear her approach. It was only when a pair of women's flat-heeled shoes came into his field of vision floorwards that he knew someone was there.

"Something wrong?" the librarian asked coldly.

"Just nits," he said.

She gasped and retreated to the safety of the charging desk to stare at him.

He combed his hair, stared right back. When her eyes would not leave his he rose and the *World Almanac* fell to the floor with a thud. He walked slowly across the floor, amused to see her eyes grow round, her face whiten. When he reached the desk, he said, "Do you have a central exchange telephone book?"

Her eyes left his long enough for her to get the book from under the counter. She slid it across to him.

"There's no need to be frightened," he said, turning to the classified section, "I'm only going to call a psychiatrist."

CHAPTER FOUR

DR. MAURICE TREFETHEN sat rocking in his chair only half listening to the tragic recital of wayward events in the life of the fat man in the armchair at the side of his desk. A youngish man of fifty, Dr. Trefethen was one of the more successful medical psychiatrists in Los Angeles, referred to by his friends as a brilliant man, by his enemies (with whom he refused to compromise) as a disgrace to his profession, mostly because of his unswerving devotion to Pavlov and the conditioned reflex theory of psychotherapy to the exclusion of everything else.

He allowed his black, wiry hair to rise in disarray from his head because he was something of a showman, believing people expected a psychiatrist to look strange, being conversant with madness as they are, and it probably accounted in part for his ability to snatch his share of trade from the faith healers who seem to gravitate to Los Angeles. That, plus *schmaltz*, which Trefethen insisted must be an essential ingredient of any contact with the public. This does not mean Trefethen was not a legitimate nor a capable psychiatrist; it only means he was realistic about competition and human needs.

Now he rose, a small man in an impeccable white smock, and the fat man rose with him. They walked to the door and Trefethen patted him encouragingly between the shoulder blades, telling him he was wasting his time worrying when he could channel such energy into something useful. "Work," he said. "That's the answer.

Whenever you feel yourself slipping into worry, start working."

"You think there's hope then, Doc?"

"Yes. Of course. Your heart hasn't given up, no? Then we won't give up either. You do what I say."

"Well…"

Dr. Trefethen clucked like a mother hen, patted the man's broad back again. The fat man looked down at the doctor as if he'd like to believe.

"You have the medicine," Trefethen said. "You take it when you feel yourself slipping, yes? It's enough until next time."

"Next Monday, then?"

"Next Monday." Trefethen nodded and pushed him gently through the door. Once the man was gone the doctor shook his head, returned to his desk, sat in his chair and entered a few notes in a meticulous hand on a card. Even as he wrote he thought: Why do they insist on telling me dreams? If they think dreams are important, they ought to go to a psychoanalyst. When he finished writing he put the card in its proper place in a drawer file, swung around in his chair to gaze out the window to weigh what he had written on the card, as he always did. Then, satisfied that what he had written was correct, he picked up the patient schedule. A free hour. He breathed with relief.

The relief was only momentary. His receptionist-secretary had heard the door to the hallway close and now she buzzed his intercom briefly. Trefethen flicked the switch. "Yes?"

"A Mr. Sherwood to see you, Doctor. He's been waiting almost an hour. I told him I thought you might see him this period. Shall I send him in?"

"Is he a referral?"

"No. Voluntary."

"All right. Send him in."

Dr. Trefethen prided himself on his analysis of patients by the way they stepped through the door to his outer office. Those first few seconds always helped establish the way it was to go, whether he should be gruff, appeasing, humorous, disinterested or any of the other manners he was capable of assuming.

When Sherwood walked in, Trefethen saw a broad-shouldered, large man of about thirty or possibly a year or two more, with untroubled, honest blue eyes, a fine, clean-cut face, neatly dressed and composed. He extended a hand and slipped smoothly into the chair at the side of the desk. The handshake was firm, the man's palms were dry, his eyes never left the doctor's face as he told him his name in a clear, well-modulated, unhesitating voice. For a moment Trefethen thought he had seen him somewhere, had heard his name before, but he dismissed it. Diagnosis: Nothing wrong with this man.

"Just what is your trouble?" Trefethen said affably. Lacking a clue as to how to proceed, it only remained for him to be himself.

"I want information more than anything else," Sherwood said. "I'm willing to pay you for your time."

"There is no trouble then with you? Is that right?" Sherwood smiled. "Before I answer that, will you answer a few questions for me?"

"All right, if you insist. But this is irregular."

"Are you required to notify the police in cases of amnesia?"

Trefethen frowned, surprised at the question. He studied Sherwood's face. It would not be Sherwood who was amnesic. Too alert. Too confident. Too much of an awareness of where he was. "No-o-o, not exactly, Mr. Sherwood. Not if the case is being handled by competent people. You know of such a case? Yes?"

"I do know of such a case, yes. But before I say anything about it, I want to know everything about amnesia."

Trefethen laughed, "Come now, Mr. Sherwood. Everythin—"

"I didn't mean that the way it sounds. What I mean is, I know nothing about it and would like to. Perhaps it would help me determine if it is a case of amnesia."

"You want to diagnose the case, with my help." Well…"

"Just what is it about amnesia you want to know?"

"I understand it can be caused by a bang on the head."

"A lot of things can be caused by a bang on the head," Trefethen said dryly. "Amnesia is only one."

Sherwood moved uncomfortably in the chair. "Can anything else cause it?"

"Amnesia," the doctor said blandly, "is not complicated. We simply do not remember unpleasant things as readily as we do pleasant ones. All of us suffer from amnesia to some degree."

"But what if a person forgets even the pleasant things, *all* the experiences for a certain period?"

Trefethen shrugged, "When an experience is a particularly trying one, a person sometimes unconsciously inhibits or 'forgets' his past difficulties up to and including it. Do you see?"

Sherwood nodded, but he wasn't ready yet to give up the idea of violence. "Could a person be hit, with no visual marks remaining and still be a victim of amnesia?"

"Possibly. There could be damage to brain cells and even severe impairment to circulation without any outward sign. Poisons can do the same thing."

"Poisons?" Sherwood said eagerly, sitting up straighter.

"Yes," Trefethen looked at Sherwood without expression.

"Does this person have amnesia yet or were you thinking of giving it to him? Or is it her?"

Sherwood smiled, "I'm not a criminal."

"Why then are you so stimulated by the thought of poison?"

"I'm not. At least not the way you think I am. I am only curious."

"Why did you come here?"

"Because, as I say, I'm curious. Now what about poisons?"

Trefethen leaned back. "Poisons can act directly on nerves to cause amnesia, yes. But there are accompanying symptoms."

"Oh." Sherwood relaxed in the chair again. Poisons were out.

"The changes in brain tissue that accompany age can cause forgetfulness, often amnesia. Is this person old?"

"No."

"Is this person about thirty-five, six feet tall, with blue eyes and black hair by any chance?"

"I prefer not to say," Sherwood said with some annoyance.

Trefethen said sharply, "I do not like discussing a phantom patient or playing guessing games. If you think there is something wrong with someone, you should take the subject to a doctor. It cannot be done through an intermediary."

"How much do you charge?"

"Twenty-five dollars an hour."

Sherwood withdrew twenty-five dollars from his billfold, put them in front of the doctor. "Now tell me anything else you know about amnesia."

Trefethen snapped his fingers. "Just like that, eh?" He looked at the money, then at Sherwood. He raised his hand as if to brush it off the desk. Then he sighed, slumped back in his chair. "All right, Mr. Sherwood, I will tell you briefly what you want to know."

"That's better."

"I'm glad you think so. There are two ways a person can have amnesia: organically or functionally. The organic way is much more common, consisting of neural languor, which renders the brain temporarily incapable of retaining and recalling stimuli. Do you understand that?"

"Yes." Sherwood settled himself comfortably in the chair, drew out a cigarette and lighted it.

"This can be caused a number of ways," the doctor continued. "Through acute infection, epileptic seizure or, say metabolic convulsion. Are you still with me, yes?"

"After a fashion, yes."

"Good. Now the functional type of amnesia is protean, but always due to the descent of an emotional block. Then comes what we term fugue, the three stages that invariably follow, though their duration is not at all standard. The first is complete dissociation, oblivescence, a state resembling somnambulism; the second is lightened oblivion where only certain facts are missing, a partial amnesia; and the third is full functioning consciousness that can come quite suddenly with all the missing parts filled in.

"The most common type of person to have an amnesic experience is the psychoneurotic, the severely so. He is sometimes constitutionally unable to withstand the rigors of reality, and the beginnings of this lie deep in the encysted complexities of the past."

"In the unconscious mind, is that it, Doctor?"

Trefethen snorted. "There is no unconscious mind."

"The subconscious, then."

"There is no subconscious either. It's all one. There is no id, ego or super-ego either. That's mumbo-jumbo talk of the witchdoctor analysts." The doctor rocked in his chair indignantly studying the wall behind Sherwood. "Does what I have told you answer your question?"

Sherwood shook his head. "I'm afraid not."

"Why?" Trefethen asked with some surprise.

"Because it doesn't tell me why I don't recall a single thing that happened during the past ten years."

The doctor stopped rocking. "Then it *is* you." He reached into a drawer and brought out a blank card. "That name that Walter Sherwood—seems a familiar one. I suppose you merely chose that. You really don't know who you are, yes?"

"No. I'm Walter Sherwood, all right. I remember everything up until May fifteenth, nineteen forty-six. This morning I woke up in a motel and found it was nineteen fifty-seven. That's all there is to it. Eleven years missing."

"How can you be sure you're Walter Sherwood? Do you have definite memories of this?"

"Of course. I remember everything in my childhood."

"You do?" Trefethen smiled thinly. "I'll bet you don't remember your third grade teacher."

"I certainly do. She was Rosemary Bush."

"Mmm. What was your principal's name?"

"Mr. Snearly. Oscar Snearly. At least until I got to the fifth grade. Then we had a man named Spencer Brewer."

"What grade did you get in freshman English in high school?"

"I got a C."

Trefethen darted him a look. "Did your folks have a car?"

"Why?"

"What was the license of it, say in nineteen thirty-four?"

Sherwood thought a moment. Then he said, "I think it was four three five seven two."

"Come now, Mr. Sherwood or whatever your name is, you don't expect me to believe that, do you?"

"You asked me, so I told you. Did you think I couldn't remember?"

"Yes."

"Why?"

"No one could possibly remember such trivia," Trefethen said calmly, stroking his chin and studying him. "Especially a person with amnesia. Just what are you up to, Mr. Sherwood?"

"Are you telling me I don't remember what I remember? It's bad enough not remembering eleven years without your trying to take away what I do remember."

Trefethen fixed him with a baleful eye. "Stop trying to fool me. You're no amnesic. If you could remember things like that you'd be a hypermnesic."

"A hyper what?"

"Never mind. It's merely the opposite of amnesia, an exaggerated degree of retention or recall." He sighed, said tiredly, "Which one of my distinguished colleagues put you up to this, anyway? I want to be in on the joke."

"Joke?" Sherwood said blankly.

"Yes, joke." Then as Trefethen looked at him, his eyes brightened with sudden remembrance. "I remember now," he said.

"Believe me, Doctor," Sherwood said earnestly, "this is no joke to me."

"I fancy not, since I just remembered where I read the name Walter Sherwood. I suppose your middle name is Evan."

"Yes," Sherwood said. "How did you know?"

"Ha!" Trefethen said, standing.

"What does that mean?"

"It means get out."

"Why?"

"Because you couldn't possibly be Walter Evan Sherwood!"

"But I am!"

"All right, prove it."

Sherwood sank back in his chair. "I can't. When I woke up this morning I found nothing but identification for a man named Morley Don Fisher in my billfold."

"I imagine," Trefethen said witheringly, no longer interested, and glancing at his desk clock. "Now if you don't mind, Mr. Fisher, I have another appointment coming up." He pushed the twenty-five dollars across the desk. "You might as well take this with you."

Sherwood stood up. "How did you know my middle name is Evan?"

"Will you get out, please?"

"I want to know."

"I happen to have a good memory, that's all." Trefethen crossed to open the hall door for him. "Now don't give me any trouble, just leave."

"But it's important to me! I want to know, I want to know what I've done for the past eleven years'!"

"You have carried the role far enough, Mr. Fisher. Now leave before I am forced to take stern measures."

There being no apparent alternative, Sherwood picked up the money and left the office.

On the way back to the motel Sherwood stopped in a cocktail lounge, hoping to find solace in the air-conditioned, plush surroundings and soft lights, a moment's respite from the puzzle so that he might go refreshed to do battle with it again. But he did not find comfort there. He ordered his drink and felt lonely and friendless among the late afternoon patrons who chattered around him, each looking and sounding so secure and confident in his life. Walter Evan Sherwood was not of this day and age; he was a man apart, a man out of time, a man transposed from his generation.

What the psychiatrist had known about him kept eating at the edge of his mind. *Would any of these people know it, too? Maybe I should have pressed Trefethen, he thought. But the doctor's look had been a menacing one and I am in a poor position to press anyone. Start pushing people around and I'll end up with the police pushing me around and wouldn't that be great?*

What was it Trefethen knew? Am I a criminal? Has he read some account of me in the paper? Maybe it's just as well he didn't believe me. He might have called the police if he had.

The drinks failed to do anything, so he left the lounge feeling lost and purposeless, returning to the motel, hoping he'd find the girl had returned. But she wasn't there, hadn't been. Things were just as he'd left them.

He lay on the bed trying to think things through, seeking a possible, positive course of action. There seemed only one and that entailed a trip halfway across the United

States, but there didn't seem to be anything else, and besides, he had the car.

He decided to take it and dozed off wondering if, when he awakened next, it would be eleven years from then, he'd be forty-eight, and it would go on and he'd be fifty-nine the next time, then seventy, eighty-one, ninety-two...one hundred and three...

CHAPTER FIVE

THE WATER BAG Sherwood had bought in Los Angeles as a safety measure in crossing the Mojave was still draped over the hood ornament when he rolled the car to a stop in the parking area in front of the administration building of Illinois Midwest College in Farrell.

The trip from the west coast had been uneventful and short, paced as it was by his sense of urgency. He had made the last run from Hastings, Nebraska, to Farrell in one jump, beginning shortly after midnight because he had only tossed and turned in the motel bed there and decided he might as well be on the road; there'd be time for sleep after he found what he had done with his life. Or would there? What if it turned out he had done something terrible? It was the thought of a possible something terrible that kept him moving. What was it the doctor had said? Some experience that made the mind refuse to accept reality, wiping out the memory? But the doctor didn't seem to think it was amnesia. Just a joke.

His entry into Farrell was that of a stranger. No one waved and there was no glimmer of recognition in anyone's eye even when he stopped downtown to ask directions to the campus—not that he expected anything, but he had been in Farrell more recently than he had Los Angeles, and though the townspeople were not apt to remember one of many students, he could not be sure, especially since he had been remembered as far away as Los Angeles by a man named Trefethen.

Sherwood turned the car northward where the school he should have recalled sprawled over the north end of the community, a composite of college and residence buildings, elm-lined streets, curved walks, looking ever so much as he imagined it, except for air conditioners that protruded from windows—he could not get used to this breaking of architectural line, the second most pronounced change in eleven years, the first being the forests of television antennas that had sprouted everywhere.

The administration building was clearly the oldest building on the campus, the face of it covered completely by ivy except where the windows were, and the broad stairs were not concrete but hewn stone that had failed through the years to keep true to the mason's level. Inside the large double doors that hissed closed behind him it was cool, a gratification after the muggy July Illinois heat, and he examined the small signs over the doors, finding the Office of Admissions and Records half way down the corridor.

The lone woman in the office rose from a far desk, slipped her glasses off her nose to let them hang on two blue ribbons from around her neck, picked up her handkerchief and came to the counter to say pleasantly, "Can I help you?"

"I'd like to take a look at my records," Sherwood said without hesitation. "My name is Walter Evan Sherwood."

She smiled. "Wouldn't you rather have a transcript? It can be easily arranged; most everyone does it. That way you don't have to wait while we look for it. We'll run it through photostat and send it wherever you like. It costs only fifty cents."

"No, I just want to look at it and take a few notes."

"That's odd, you know," she said, moving away to a large filing cabinet. "Most people just send letters and a money order or check. Not very many come to look up the records personally."

"I started in nineteen forty-six," he said helpfully. And he had a thought: Suppose I have no record here? Suppose I didn't go to school at all?

"It doesn't make any difference. We file them all alphabetically. Sherwood, is it? Let's see." She drew out a drawer. "It ought to be easy to find. Sheldon, Sheldon, Shelley, Shenton…Mmm…Sheridan. That's more like it. Sherman, Sherman, Sherman. Never knew we had so many Shermans. Sherwood. There. No. That's Perry Sherwood. Ah, here we are. Walter Sherwood. Walter Evan Sherwood." She withdrew the folder and carried it to the counter. "Pre-Med. I suppose you're a doctor now."

"Thank you," he said, taking the card and not wanting to commit himself, eager to have a look at it.

"You understand you're not to take the card out of the office."

"I understand," he said, nodding, wishing she would leave him, absorbed in the paper.

Walter Evan Sherwood had started the first semester 1946-1947 at Midwest with Chemistry 102, Hygiene 101, English 101, Zoology 101, Physical Education and Math 114, and for a moment he was sad to think of his not remembering any of it. His grades were excellent, too, with only a single B, and that in English. Well, he had never cared much for gerunds and ablatives and parsing. But he was surprised by the good marks nonetheless.

The second semester 1946-1947 was much like the first, with a more advanced chemistry, inorganic and qualitative analysis, trigonometry, English again and comparative vertebrate anatomy, and the grades were all A's. *Quite a student, this Walter Sherwood*, he mused.

He looked for the first semester 1947-1948, found instead the summer semester 1947, and thought: *I didn't rest in the summer, did I, I wonder why I was in such a hell of a hurry why did I get nothing but A's didn't I have a social life or anything to interfere? Now why was I running like that?*

He looked down the column. It ended with the summer of 1948, with vertebrate embryology. What then? That only represented three years of work. He looked up into the eyes of the woman.

"Are you really Mr. Sherwood?" she asked.

"Why do you ask that?"

"If you're not, I shouldn't be letting you see those records."

"Well, I am."

"You were looking at them as if you'd never seen them before, as if you never heard of this Sherwood.

"Sometimes," he said, "I wish I never had." And when she laughed and he knew he had convinced her, he put the card down. "Looking at this record only brings back how hard I worked, packing three years' work in two years. I should have finished the four years." He sighed with a weariness he did not feel and waited for her to take the bait.

"That would have been silly," she said. "Sure, you could have gotten your B. S., but that's all. You should be happy you transferred out." She ran a polished fingernail under the card, picked it up and inserted it in the folder. "Too many of them just put in their four years and that's it, no direction, no goal, just getting a degree and going on from there. At least you knew where you were going."

"Yes," he said lightly. "Thank God for that." Come on, come on, tell me what I want to know.

"Did you do as well in medical school?"

"Oh, yes." He felt the sweat begin, not wanting to be at this disadvantage, seeking a way to turn it so she'd give him information instead, trying to smile extravagantly and knowing it was only a shadow of a grin. "By the way, do you have it recorded where I went? I mean, I want the record straight."

She opened the folder and nodded. "I'm sure this is right."

What is it? he wanted to scream.

"Ryerson Medical in Chicago?"

"That's right."

Sherwood thanked her and left the building, buoyant with a sense of real accomplishment. May 15, 1946, was no longer the end of the Walter Sherwood he knew. He had traced himself through the summer of 1948. Oh, he hadn't done any more than establish the fact that he had gone to Midwest for two years, but at least that was definite. The little things, the place (or places) he lived, the things be did, his extracurricular activities, the people he knew, loved, hated, tolerated, argued with, the people who made up his life for those two years at Midwest were at the moment unimportant compared with the larger information, the picture of his entire life, the joining together of the two threads, the one dangling in a room in a house on Dahlia Drive in Los Angeles on May 15, 1946, and which now dangled provocatively at the end of summer in 1948, and the other end of the thread which lay loose and untied in a motel on Colorado Boulevard in July, 1957.

The threads must be joined, had to be joined before he could feel a whole man. There would be time for filling in, for putting the flesh on the bones, later.

Webster, Illinois, was only a jog off the route to Chicago from Farrell, so Sherwood abandoned the good road to turn off on an older, cracked highway to the small town. He would have rather continued on to Chicago, but with Webster so close he felt he should visit it to see where Morley Don Fisher was supposed to live, telling himself he'd be wise to be careful and unobtrusive because he didn't know what Webster knew of Mr. Fisher and for all he knew there might be a warrant out for his arrest.

The town was one of those that had flourished in the days of the horse-drawn vehicle, being midway between a certain number of larger communities, thriving with the advent of the motorcar, but withering on the vine with the coming of larger, straighter highways and belt lines, bypassed and forgotten, trains no longer stopping at the old station, the stores run down, the streets bumpy and badly in the need of repair.

Sherwood drove through the two-block business district, then started to circle it, looking for Summit Avenue. He found an old wooden street sign that designated it, started west, noting the numbers as he went. They stopped with 508. There was simply nothing beyond it except a railroad crossing and the beginning of a cornfield. He went down the rutted road for more than a mile, not finding a house.

There was, then, no 1213 Summit Avenue.

He turned around, followed the street to the business section. There was no continuation of Summit Avenue on the other side of town.

Morley Don Fisher did not live at 1213 Summit Avenue in Webster, Macon County, Illinois, because there was no 1213.

And also because, more probably, there was no Morley Don Fisher, he told himself.

He toyed with the idea of inquiring at the post office, but decided against it. He was too close to Chicago and what he could find at the Ryerson Medical School to jeopardize what might happen if he got out of the car in Webster.

Still, the puzzle of Fisher and the fictitious address kept gnawing at his mind, and he wished he could put it in place along with the other unsolved parts, fitting them together as a whole and seeing it all at once and making sense out of it.

He saw Ryerson Medical School in the bright light of the next morning, a time-worn brick building on Chicago's north side, a point equidistant to a half dozen hospitals, though it was Wright Memorial that was the training ground for the student personnel, and it looked like anything but what he thought a medical school should, an office building with its fluorescent lighting perhaps, or a hospital, even a small factory was conceivable, but there was no denying the chiseled-in-stone Roman letters that told what it was above the columns to either side of the entranceway.

Sherwood stood across the street from it for a while, watching several groups of young men and women with books under their arms coming and going, chatting as they moved on the road steps, and he felt alien, not moved by the inner compulsion of this other life he'd had, and feeling he was a stranger about to inquire into the history of someone else, a creature long dead and forgotten, but finding it necessary to take this step because it was all part of the job now, to fit this in with the rest, not knowing what he would find, suddenly not caring too much because this was so foreign to his nature now.

He moved across the street like any other man, moving up the steps now as the others had, passing the portals he surely must have passed countless time before, knowing he was closer to what he was seeking, that there might even be recognition here in this busy place, seeing the high ceilings and walls, the cleanliness of it, and the smells he associated with things medical, thinking my but this is an old place but I suppose its age has nothing to do with what's taught here.

"Dr. Sherwood!"

Sherwood looked at several faces before he saw him, a fair-sized, black-haired man with a ruddy face, heavy eyebrows and glasses, wearing a gray smock with pencils and instruments in a breast pocket beneath which was stitched in a label bearing the words *Max Rankel*.

The grinning man extended a long hand from the smock sleeve as he approached, and when Sherwood took it he pumped it hard. "Where've you been, Walt? You dropped out of here as if you didn't know us. How've you been?"

"All right…Max, isn't it?"

"You're dam right," Rankel said, slapping his upper arm heartily. "Don't tell me you'd forget old Rankel that easy now, bud. Gee, you look good. Whatever you're doing must agree with you."

"It has, Max. Nice to see you again."

"Come on, come on, what're you doing here, anyway? You know not many ever get enough time to come back." He chuckled. "Maybe most of them are too damn glad to get the hell out of here, eh?"

"Oh, I don't know," Sherwood said indefinitely. "I thought I'd come around and take a look at my records. Might bring back some of the old times," he said truthfully, trying to fit Rankel's mood and wondering how best to use it.

"They can do that any old time in the office. This calls for a celebration." He looked at a wall clock and groaned. "And there's all day yet and I can't take off because of the end of summer work. Look, what're you doing for lunch? We could run down to Amy's—"

"Well, there are a few things I have to do, Max."

"Sounds like old Sherwood, always on the go. Tell you what, Walt, there's a class this morning, we're working on three dogs, perineorrhaphy and all that for the catheter deal in this section—you know the routine. I'll be there until about eleven, so let me know."

Sherwood smiled, not making heads or tails of what he was talking about. "Maybe you can do one thing for me before you go, Max."

"Sure, Walt. Name it, boy."

"Which of my old instructors do you think I ought to see first?"

"Are you kidding? Old Booey's been heartsick since you left like that. He had you figured for an assistantship, you know. You'd better go on up and see him."

"Where's he at now, Max?"

"Still the same place." He darted a look at the clock. "I got to be sailing. Damn fools're apt to weigh out enough nembutal to put those dogs away for keeps if I'm not there to steady their grubby little hands." He moved down the ball, saying over his shoulder, "Don't forget now."

Sherwood turned away, wondering who Rankel was and what he did at Ryerson, certain he had in him at least one source of information if all the others failed. He found the office, met a woman who chatted indifferently while she produced his records, and looked them over.

Medicine, physiology, histology, pathology, micro-anatomy, minor surgery, major surgery, clinical medicine, and a host of others, some of them hardly pronounceable, and all A's. Once again he marveled at the Sherwood that was and the drive that had been his, never letting up, moving to Ryerson from Midwest, plunging right in during the fall of 1948, working without ceasing through the spring of 1951.

"You should be proud of that record, Doctor," the woman was saying. "Not many of them manage to go through the way you did."

"Thanks," he said, moving the forms across the counter to her and wondering exactly what she meant. He could see he got through in a hurry, but that was no change from Midwest. "Can you tell me where I'll find Dr. Booey?"

"Oh, he's not been changed."

Why did they insist on putting it that way? "Would you mind telling me just where that is?" he asked, deciding to chance the direct question.

"Why, third floor south," she said, giving him a puzzled look.

"Thanks."

CHAPTER SIX

SHERWOOD FOUND Dr. Booey where the office girl said he would, but of course he did not know at first it was Dr. Booey, this man he saw lecturing to the crowded classroom, his back to anatomy charts on the wall. The lecturing man gave him one glance, said something to the class Sherwood could not hear, put his pointer on the desk and walked through the door to the hallway to him.

"Walter," he said without emotion or expression, hardly moving his thick lips. He was a smooth-faced, rosy-cheeked man with wisps of hair on his otherwise bald head, looking at him steadily with bright gray eyes.

"Dr. Booey?"

The faint outcrop of white hairs that passed for eyebrows rose a little and there was frank puzzlement in the eyes. Then something happened behind the eyes and the man turned to the doorway and said, "Mr. Scott, if you please." A man rose from a desk in the far corner of the room, moved to the anatomy chart with a pointer. Then Dr. Booey started down the hall, saying, "Come along."

Sherwood followed him to a small, book-filled office where the doctor turned on the small plate beneath a small coffee pot before he turned to face him, studying him for a long moment before he said, "Sit down," and sat himself behind a desk. Then he said gravely, "You didn't know me out there?"

Sherwood sensed a power in this man, a strength that engendered trust. There had been no affectionate greeting, no shaking of hands, not even a smile, yet he felt the doctor's concern. Sherwood said, "No, I didn't know you."

The eyes shifted somewhere inside the man, like lenses moving out of sight, and their brightness increased. Sherwood felt as if he were being resected on the spot. The doctor said, "When did it happen?"

"I don't know."

Booey's eyes slid away. "I knew it would happen some day. You were hardly ready."

Sherwood flushed. "I'm afraid I don't know what you are talking about."

"I suppose not." Booey sighed. "We all wondered when it would come. You were always so tense, so…overly dedicated. It didn't seem natural to any of us."

"I stopped at the office and saw my record. I worked pretty hard, I guess."

"How much do you remember?"

Sherwood's eyes fell before those of the doctor who knew so much about him, and he studied his hands. "Eleven years is missing."

"Eleven *years?*"

Sherwood jerked his head up, looked at the doctor squarely. "I can't remember anything after May fifteenth, nineteen forty-six." Suddenly he was sick of hearing it, thinking it, living it, saying it, wishing he could hand it to this man to struggle with.

"Yes, you can," the doctor said.

"What?"

"You can remember our meeting in the hall."

"Well, yes."

"So you do remember some things. How far back does this go? If you knew the day…"

"I can remember back to July eleventh. I woke up in a motel in Los Angeles, remembering nothing for the previous eleven years."

Booey was surprised. "That's very strange, not remembering over such a long period." He shook his head. "A pity, too. You were a brilliant man, did you know that? One of the best. Maybe that's it. Maybe you were too brilliant. But as I say, many of us saw it coming. It seemed to be just a question of time." The coffee hissed behind him and he twisted in his chair, brought out two mugs and set them side by side on the desk and poured the steaming coffee.

"What do you mean about it being a question of time?"

Booey shrugged. "You ran through here like a man possessed, grabbed your Doctor of Medicine on the fly, then settled down for a research on a fellowship in neurophysiology, if you can call shutting the door of a room on everything else settling down. You did that here. You were known as the Ryerson Recluse."

The doctor picked up the mug, blew across the top of the coffee, sipped it. "You were like a wire with a turnbuckle at either end that you kept tightening. The wire was bound to break some time."

"You think I've cracked up," Sherwood said dismally.

"What else is there to think, considering your not remembering things, the classic flight from reality? I don't suppose you remember why you were running."

"Running?"

"Your dedication, the thing that makes what happened to you so transparent. It was your father and your experience with the medical corps in the army. You were obsessed with mental aberration and you were dedicated to doing something about it. You felt that if you understood the mind you might find a way to prevent such a thing, and you seemed to think you were the only man in the world working toward that end." The doctor drank a little of the coffee and said gravely, "I think it's obvious now that you were only racing against your own disintegration and that you lost the race. Don't think me cruel, Walter, but there seems to be no other way to explain your condition."

Sherwood said nothing, feeling himself sinking into a morass of bewilderment, seeing himself as a man running after his own shadow, a man who caught glimpses of his real self only out of the corners of his eyes. He thought: *so this is insanity!* Then he caught himself at the edge of the precipice and struggled back to reason and said thickly, "I'm not insane, Doctor," and made himself look Booey straight in the eye. "I don't care what you think, I'm not off my rocker."

"Have you had an examination?"

"I've been to a psychiatrist."

"What did he say?"

"Dr. Trefethen thought I was playing a joke on him. He said because I could remember my early days so well I couldn't have amnesia."

Booey snorted. "He should go back to school. None of us can be sure about anything, least of all about things as nebulous as the brain." After a moment he said quietly, "It's ironic. The brain was your specialty."

There was a pause, with Sherwood in a flush studying his hands again, Booey's eyes on his face.

"You can take heart, however," Booey said. "If it's a simple amnesia you stand a chance of coming out of it. Even neuroses have a built-in self-limiting factor. Usually two years. For better or worse." After another pause the doctor said gently, "You and I were close, Walter. As close as student and teacher could be. You saw things quickly and you were—well, damn interested, which is something few of the gooks we see here really are." He added almost affectionately, "You never thought there was too much to learn," and after a pause said, "What ever made you come to see me, Walter?"

"I was following a thread. I met a man in the hall with a label on his pocket that said he was Max Rankel. He greeted me like a long lost brother and when I asked him whom I ought to look up, he suggested you."

"Max was a good friend of yours," Booey said, nodding. "A sort of balance wheel for you." Then he said firmly, "Walter, you'll have to have treatment. There are ways of getting around what's wrong with you. Hypnosis, for example. Helps fill in the missing areas until the mind accepts the reality that was."

Sherwood shook his head. "No, I'm not undergoing any treatment until I find out everything. I know roughly what happened between nineteen forty-six and nineteen fifty-one. I've followed it that far. I'll have to bring it up to date. Then if it all doesn't come back I'll start treatment."

"You say you don't remember anything prior to your waking up in a motel in Los Angeles?"

"Yes."

"What were you doing there?"

"I don't know…I grew up out there."

"You used to talk about it in the rare times you did any talking. But it was your father that bothered you mostly, as I've said. That, plus the business of the army. Anyway, when you got out you decided one night to become a doctor, a brain specialist, and once you got started nothing could stop you. You loved medicine, lived medicine, breathed it, married it. Evidently you finally pushed yourself too far." Booey looked sourly into his coffee cup, swirled the grounds. "It could have happened to any of us under the same circumstances."

"I wish," Sherwood said crisply, "that you wouldn't talk as if I were out on pass from an asylum."

Booey looked at him sharply.

Sherwood went on, "I think you're wrong. I don't think it's anything at all like that. There are some odd things about it. Except for the eleven missing years, everything else is normal. Too normal, it seems to me."

"Odd things, Walter? What odd things?"

Sherwood told him in detail about waking up with the girl in the room, about the billfold and the name he found in it, the fact that there was no such address as 1213 Summit Avenue in Webster.

"I'm not so far gone that I couldn't follow the thread here, Doctor Booey. And I saw with my own eyes there was no house in Webster. Then there is the matter of accounting for my complete physical description on the papers in my billfold. Try explaining that."

"It does have strange overtones," Booey conceded. "That is, if everything you say is true."

"It's all true."

The doctor scowled at Sherwood for a long moment, then rose from the chair, shoved it into the desk and put his hands on the back of it, staring down at him. "I must confess you don't talk like a man with amnesia."

"How am I supposed to talk?"

"You're too aware of your surroundings, Walter. You're too aware of what you're doing and who you are. Let me ask you something: "Did you know who you were when you woke up out there in the motel?"

"Of course."

"Then you looked at the billfold and saw the name Fisher?"

"Yes."

"You didn't think you were this Fisher?"

"No. Not for a minute."

Booey nodded. "That's where it doesn't jibe. A true amnesic wouldn't have known who he was. He'd have been convinced he was Fisher." He squinted his eyes in thought. "This Trefethen may have had a point. You remember some things too well. You follow a thread too well."

"And I'll continue following it past Ryerson, Doctor."

Booey nodded. "Maybe the real Sherwood isn't gone after all. You've got to know, you say. Well, that's what you always used to say." He smiled now for the first time and Sherwood saw his horse teeth. Booey sat down, reached into a drawer, brought out an ashtray and a pack of cigarettes. "Let's have a smoke on your analytical mind, Dr. Sherwood, for you are a doctor, you know, even though your interest lies in neurophysiology." He passed the pack over. "And let's hope your probing pierces that hidden area of your mind. I'll help you all I can."

"Dr. Trefethen said something I didn't understand," Sherwood said. "He said he suddenly remembered my name from somewhere. At the time I thought maybe I had made headlines or something."

Booey gestured to include all the books and magazines on the shelves. "Where else but in a journal? Psychological Abstracts, Journal of Psychiatric Quarterly, EEG Journal, a dozen bulletins. You were always writing about something, stirring things. You were an upstart. Not too many agreed with you, though they listened.

Maybe this Trefethen read something of yours he didn't like." He reached over, ran a thick finger down a stack of publications, pulled one out, thumbed through it studiously, found what he was looking for and shoved it across the desk to Sherwood, saying, "There's one."

Sherwood glanced at an article entitled, "Certain Aspects of the Integrative Action of the Nervous System," and it was bylined "Dr. Walter Evan Sherwood." Another one Booey threw at him concerned Sherwood's views on the Rahm Stimulator, whatever that was, and still another was entitled, "An Exploration of the Parietal Cortex and Its Somaesthetic Sensitivity."

He shook his head. "It means nothing to me."

"Of course it doesn't. Not now. But doesn't it help you to know you did it?"

Sherwood considered it, then said, "I'm not sure. It makes me feel maybe the loss is too great, that I'll never make it back."

"Don't you suppose you still have it?"

Sherwood said dubiously, "I don't know."

"Well, you do," Booey said, tapping his forehead. "There are two hemispheres for remembering: each of the temporal lobes, each with an equal value for retention. One of them can be removed without evidence of marked memory loss or interference with the capacity of perceptual interpretation. So you're doubly insured. Only temporarily short-circuited."

"I hope you're right."

Booey's eyes narrowed ever so little. "There is one great difference between you and me at the moment."

"What's that?"

"I know I'm right," he said evenly.

"And I, in my condition, cannot be sure," Sherwood said miserably. "Is that it?"

"That is a matter of fact. But I wouldn't let that self-pity creep in there. It doesn't become you. It can even defeat you."

Sherwood knew Booey was right. He must not bewail the man he had been, must not think of possible failure. In fact, there could be no real failure, for he could start all over again at Midwest, couldn't he? Couldn't he move right up to Ryerson again? The same man taking the same courses because he had forgotten them? It wouldn't make sense to anyone else, but it was a possible route if he should finally fail to lift the curtain of his mind.

There was something else. All during the talk with Booey he had a feeling of increased unreality, and he had only discovered in the last few moments why. Booey was talking to him as if he had known him for years, which he had, acting on the basis of a friendship long ago formulated by a Sherwood that Sherwood himself didn't even know, talking to him easily, without guile, as a friend, while Sherwood could only answer as a stranger, thinking as a stranger. That was the unreality and the reason for it.

Booey was saying, "Of course you'll want to know what you did when you left here; that's natural. Well, I wish I could help you, but I can't tell you very much. I have your address here in a book somewhere." Booey shifted papers on his desk, lifting books and paperweights, finally picking up a red leather notebook and flicking its pages. "Here it is. Three forty-seven Walnut Street, Merrittville, Michigan."

"Michigan?"

Hooey slanted a look at him. "That mean something to you?"

"No. I was surprised. I wonder how I ever got there."

"And what you were doing there, which is more important." Booey sighed, put the book down. "You left here in a hurry at the end of nineteen fifty-one. Earlier I had received some inquiries about you from some department of the government. I think it was the Investigation Division of the Civil Service Commission, or one of the other departments."

When Sherwood looked puzzled, he went on, "Such inquiries have become a general thing, Walter. An executive order created a federal employee loyalty program in nineteen forty-seven for critical positions. You had applied for such a position or someone—certainly not I— referred your name to a government agency. All I know is you left here for research, but just exactly what it was I don't know, though it would be in your specialty, of course. I was sorry to see you go."

"Max mentioned something about how you thought I might stay on for an assistantship."

"It was a blow when you left, but I recovered."

"So I started working for a secret government project somewhere. Is that right?"

"Secret?" Booey grunted in amusement. "I doubt it. There's not much secrecy in medical research; it's a lot different from atomic research, unless of course it would be in a vital area of defense or attack, and I rather doubt that. You probably worked on something that interested you very much, something like an exact measurement of electrical impulses along a nerve. You had a flair for combining electronics and neurology. They are similar, in a way."

"But even though I was doing research that interested me, I'd still be working for the government?"

"Not necessarily. In Merrittville, Michigan, there is a research center not far from town, I understand, but nobody knows very much about it. At least not me. And not because it's so secret or anything like that. It's simply because it's in such an out-of-the-way place half way between Traverse City and Frankfort, up there near Michigan's little finger, which is exactly why it was placed there away from the beaten track, so it would be quiet and fellows like you could get your work done. I fancy it is rather well-equipped. It's run by a man named Schlessenger. Don't know much about him."

"I should have invited you up there," Sherwood said, smiling. "It's the least I could have done after what you must have done for me down here."

"You did, but we could never get together on the date; you know how that is. I was frankly curious about your work, but you never wrote about that. My guess is you were either working on a graduate fellowship or on an outright grant from the National Science Foundation, or for one of the research outfits for the armed forces, maybe even for the Department of Defense itself, bypassing the services. It's a toss-up which one, though I think the latter ones are hardly likely."

Booey folded a piece of paper absently. "I know a lot of men who are quite happy with research. I've had temptations myself. There are a lot of theories of mine I'd like to go into, but like a newspaperman who has an idea for a book he never gets written, I never get around to working on anything strictly my own. I feel I owe something to these knuckleheads we get in here every year, I guess. If everybody was doing research, there'd be nobody left to teach the kids. Then where'd we be?"

"Well," Sherwood said, "that seems to settle what happened to me after Ryerson."

"For a while it wasn't so nice in research," Booey went on. "It was touch and go when the Senate subcommittees started to ferret out anyone who had ever heard of Karl Marx. But there is more freedom now. It turned out nearly everybody had heard the name at some time or other. More coffee?"

"No, thanks. I'd like to have that address and be on my way. It looks like the answer to everything."

"Here," Booey said, tearing off an unused sheet of paper. "I'll write it down for you. I don't envy you going up there, a place you don't even remember."

"Maybe it will come back to me."

"Like Ryerson has?" Booey shook his head. "I doubt it. I want you to come back here if things don't work out, Walter. I know a lot of good men who might do you some good."

"If I run into a dead end," Sherwood promised, taking the paper Booey had folded so neatly for him, "I'll be back."

"I won't count on it. You may only find Merrittville is a jumping off place for somewhere else. You said you woke up in Los Angeles with somebody else's identification."

"It's a chance I'll have to take."

"I got a letter or two from you after you got up there, but I threw them away, as I always do, after I answer them, and I'll confide I always have a backlog, too. It seems you mentioned once going deep-sea fishing in Grand Traverse Bay and catching a twenty-three pound Muskie and at the time I thought it was fine you were finding time to do things like that."

Booey chuckled as if at some secret thought. "Just like when you went fishing through the ice on Crystal Lake in the dead of winter. That surprised me, too. You sent me a picture of the inside of your cabin—they put them on skids and tow them out on the lake, you said—and you and your wife looked—"

"My...*wife?*"

"Of course." Then Booey was suddenly agitated. "My God, that's right, you don't remember, do you?"

CHAPTER SEVEN

FOR A LONG TIME Virginia Appleby sat in bed, the covers hunched up under her chin, staring at the little hallway where the man had gone out, and from out of the muddled depths of her mind where a thousand questions fought to impinge themselves on her consciousness emerged the most important one: *Who was he?* Immediately her orderly mind set about to solve this question for her. The man was not John Trankle. Yet the last time she had been in a man's room it had been the room of John Trankle and the early morning sun rising over Lake Michigan was sending an exploring finger of yellow through a window, brightening the flowered wallpaper on the opposite wall just over John Trankle's head. She had stayed the night to help with his lessons, she in the only cushioned chair in the room and he on the floor across the room, his head against the wall.

"Plantaris," she had said, and he tried, "Ah...origin, femur at outer bifurcation of linea aspera...ah...posterior ligament of knee..." and it was as if he had said it only a moment ago. But of course it had been only yesterday.

Then came the pain, she remembered, when she had tried to get out of the chair, and John had helped her to the bathroom because she was so suddenly sick and he was so solicitous because she had stayed up all night to see that he learned all he'd need for the final exam. Then came the hospital.

"Blood count?" she remembered asking the doctor.

"Whites around fifteen thousand."

And she said, "Leukocytes working overtime. Should have known better than to associate with a medical student. Where's the infection, Doctor, appendix?"

The doctor had told her she was right and they had agreed on the operation for the next morning...

No, this man who had just left the room was not John Trankle. This was not the room where she had helped him cram for his anatomy final, these were not the walls that echoed to plantaris, longus capitis, quadratus femoris and all the rest. This place had monk's cloth drapes at the windows, wall-to-wall carpeting, original art on the walls, and not art John Trankle would have chosen. She had the feeling they were not pictures a man would select. In fact, the whole place did not have any real maleness about it, least of all any John Trankle bachelor maleness, which helped her decide it was not the apartment of the man she had seen depart from it, whoever he might be.

Now from the caldron of churning thoughts that was her mind came a single, bright picture complete with feelings: The doctor was going out the door and she could see the starched whiteness of his coat as he turned and smiled as he glanced at his wristwatch and she asked what time it was. "Going somewhere?" he said. "A little after nine." And a host of little pictures that followed in quick succession: a nurse and thermometer, nurse and pill, white ceiling and lights out and the yellow effulgence of the corridor baseboard lights. All that had been only last night, yesterday when she fell ill in John Trankle's apartment and she had been taken to the hospital and after much probing and talking they had decided it was appendicitis, and the operation had been planned for the following morning. This morning. *Today.*

Virginia threw the covers down and stared at the nakedness of her abdomen. The scar was there. The operation had been done. Long ago.

How long ago?

She felt the anxiety start in her arms and legs. Before it could move anywhere else she swung her feet out of bed to the floor. Quickly she picked, up a robe draped across a chair.

The bathroom was genuine tile. She glanced in the mirror, was startled to see the mature woman who returned her gaze. She turned on the side and overhead lights for a better look at herself, saw a face no longer as thin as it was yesterday; it had a lot more character now, and it pleased her to see that it was a happy face without a single worry line. She inspected her teeth, observed that she had taken good care of them, examined the rest of herself, was not displeased to find that the thinness that had so often worried her was gone. A thought kept intruding in the forepart of her brain: These things do not happen overnight.

She returned to the living room-bedroom and sat on the bed. Just how was it possible to take a sedative one night and wake up a long time later in some apartment somewhere? It wasn't possible that was all there was to it. Not *normally* possible. And instantly all the conversations on mental aberrations she had ever given ear to in school flooded her mind. Just what had gone wrong?

Virginia drew up a knee and clasped her hands over it, wondering why she wasn't frightened now. She decided it was because of her academic training and a slavish adherence to the scientific method. Where there is an action there will be an equal and opposite reaction, wasn't that it? There have to be enough plusses to take care of all the minuses. So there has to be an answer of sorts and something insanity is the answer, it is an answer of sorts and something can be done about it. We could start from there and work toward the light.

She tried to go back, to shatter the veil over her mind, but she could not. All she could see was the face of the doctor when she told him she wanted to have the operation, the serene face of the nurse who brought in her pill, her sedative. No placebo, that pill. It blotted out the interim. Maybe I've been unconscious ever since and people have had to feed me intravenously. But no, my muscles, the dear old plantaris and the thousands of others, would have atrophied by this time. All that remained would be nerves. She smiled, imagining herself nothing but a heap of bones with nerves running every which way in a spider-web of threads.

Such imaginings were a part of Virginia Appleby. She had inherited it, together with a lively curiosity (from your grandfather, dear, her mother had told her, not from either of us). Her first curiosity had been the milk separator that she had seen her father use with regularity on the farm, the silver-painted monstrosity on the back porch. Something magical happened to the milk in among the humming, spinning things inside the machine, and though her father did his best to explain it, he was not able to answer satisfactorily just why one liquid could weigh more than another. This was finally settled one day when he presented her with a University of Illinois farm bulletin on milk separation he had sent for. She read it fascinatedly.

"Now that you know all about it," her father said when she finished, "you can go turn the handle."

For some reason it never seemed quite as magical after that.

Then there was the veterinarian who came around, a little embarrassed by her curiosity in his every move, and he cast many an uneasy glance at her father during some of his more basic, surgical functions. But her father invariably shrugged it off.

Virginia did not get the answers to these things—not the detailed, scientific answers she wanted—until her curiosity had taken her from the farm to college in Chicago. She was happy in her objectivity, in her detached view of things, the attitude of the scientists, as she studied microbiology, cytochemistry and pathogenic bacteriology, and helped others along the way—John Trankle, for example.

As she rose now, knowing that she could not sit on the bed all day—though it was a relief from class—she spied the telephone in the corner. That was an answer. She could call Sylvia Lipscomb, one of the few girls in immunology and one of her best friends, if Sylvia was home at this hour. She had momentarily forgotten her schedule. Or she might even give John Trankle a ring. Or the school itself. But what would she say? I just woke up in an apartment I don't know where and saw a man I don't know just go out the door?

She approached the phone, wanting to call someone. But this one had no dial, and she frowned at it. All telephones in Chicago were supposed to have dials, weren't they?

She picked up the receiver to listen. No dial tone. But, of course, no dial.

"Yes?" A man's voice. She nearly dropped the phone in surprise. Now why—

"Yes?" the voice demanded.

"Uh—" She cleared her throat. "Can you tell me what time it is, please?" she asked, not knowing what else to say.

"A quarter after ten. Did your clock stop?"

"Oh, I forgot." Now she saw the built-in electric clock on the wall. "Thank you." Who was she talking to? When there was no sound of a break in connection, she further took advantage of the voice by asking boldly, "What day is this?"

"Day?"

"Yes."

"Wednesday."

It had been Wednesday night when she had gene to sleep to wake up on Thursday after the operation.

"I mean the date," she said.

"Oh. The fifteenth. July fifteenth."

"July?" she asked, trying to keep the quaver out of her voice.

"Yes. July." The voice sounded a little annoyed. "Nineteen forty-six?"

The voice chuckled. "Fifty-seven, you mean."

"Oh, yes."

"Is that ail?"

"Yes. Thank you."

She dropped the phone softly into the cradle and stared at it, feeling a vague anxiety again. Eleven years was an awfully long time not to remember anything. She hadn't thought she was missing that much. Why, she'd be through school then, John Trankle would be a doctor now and Sylvia would be married and have all those kids she wanted.

But what about Virginia Appleby? Don't forget her.

I'm not forgetting her. As a matter of fact, I'm very concerned about her. And that man. Why, that man who left here…he could be…my husband. She said "my husband" and the words had a strange ring to them and she felt the beginnings of a blush. She pulled the robe more tightly round her and moved to the bureau because she saw a woman's white knit bag there. She undid the drawstring.

Inside were a billfold, a keycase with two keys she had never seen before, lipstick, handkerchief, two sticks of gum, half a package of mints, gold pen and pencil, compact. The billfold contained a few dollars, her driver's license—no, wait. The license was for someone else. A Mrs. Morley Don Fisher. She read it through, found the description tallied with hers, accepted at once the fact that she must be Mrs. Fisher, who lived, the license said, in Webster, Illinois.

She took up the man's billfold, took out the driver's license. The man was obviously her husband, Morley Don Fisher.

Virginia put her hands on the cold top of the bureau to steady herself. There could be no denying she was his wife, not with this evidence. But she didn't want to be his wife. How could you love somebody you didn't even know, much less…

She must not be there when he came back. Must not be! He hadn't taken his billfold or anything else because he didn't intend to be gone long, so he'd be back soon, so there was need to hurry. She had to think about this, had to get away from here and think and work it out. She had his address, she'd contact him if she decided to, later on. Right now the main thing was to get out of there and get out fast.

Money. She'd need money. If he were her husband, then there would be no crime in using some of his money, if he had any. But she had seen the green in his billfold and now she withdrew a wad of bills from it, counting one hundred and eighty-three dollars. She couldn't take all he had; that wouldn't be right. Then she saw the book of Traveler's Checks. There were eight one-hundred dollar checks in there, so he needn't worry about money. So she took the one hundred and eighty-three dollars from his billfold and added it to those in her own.

Next she scurried about the place, made the bed (I just can't leave it like this, I don't care if I am using precious time) and she folded his pajamas neatly on the chair. In the storage compartment she found dresses and a suitcase along with all Mr. Fisher's things. She packed her clothes, hardly noticing what they were—though she could see they weren't cheap things—she was in such a hurry. She would have liked to have taken a leisurely bath—or even a quick bath—but the thought of Mr. Fisher walking in on her was just too much.

She had a few agonized moments when she stood still in the middle of the room toying with the idea of writing him a note, explaining what had happened to her, but she thought if he was really her husband he'd be more worried with a note than without one. He might even go to the police and she'd be stopped and then they'd be reunited before she had a chance to get used to the idea of being married. If she didn't leave a note he'd think she had become angry or something; at least he'd not get the police involved. Not at first, anyway.

When everything was ready she gave a final inspection to the rooms, picked up her suitcase and, after one final glance around, went through the door and slammed it after her, stepping out into the warm, brilliant sun.

CHAPTER EIGHT

ALL OF THE Appleby farm, one of the prettiest in northern Illinois, could be seen from a rise in the blacktop road to the south of it, the gray ribbon of road dipping down and running cleanly by it without even a faint whisper of a curve, and disappearing in distant greenery. Homer Appleby, who had inherited the land from his father, even as his father had inherited it before him, had dedicated his life to keeping it neat and spotless, even to planting everything, which he did in rows laid out with a mathematician's precision.

The house and outbuildings, nestling in a forest of green elms, were painted a bright white to match the white crushed rock driveway that ran to the yard. The farm's picture book effect was further enhanced by white wood fencing which Appleby painted every other year. Wood fencing was a little unusual in that area, but Appleby had once seen a Kentucky farm with such fencing and could not rest until he had put it up everywhere on his farm.

When Virginia saw it from the rise that July she saw at once the elms had grown so huge they almost blotted out the view of the house itself from this point, and she at once recalled that her grandfather had planted those very trees and only wished now that he were alive to see what he had wrought.

The taxi, of course, did not stop for the view but hurried on down the blacktop, the meter clicking away, Virginia in a wretched state of expectation and anxiety. She had not wanted to telephone, to communicate in any way because to recite what had happened would sound ridiculous and impossible and would only arouse anxiety. Now she was not so sure she had been right. What if her parents were dead? It would have been better to know a thing like that before coming here. What if they had moved? Retired to town? After all, she knew her father would not be able to work the farm forever, even if he had been in perfect health the last time she remembered seeing him.

The car swung into the white lane and down it to the yard and Virginia got out, the driver getting her suitcases, and she wondered what they would think, seeing her come in like this, if they were still there, and when the taxi man had been paid and still hesitated before he got into the car, she had an impulse to ask him to wait until she tried the door or saw someone. But she waved him on and stood in the yard looking at the house, seeing no face at the windows, only little changes here and there, the memory of other days washing over her.

There was no one home, she discovered. The car was gone, and she remembered suddenly it was Monday and of course they wouldn't be home. They always took their eggs to market on Monday and did their shopping and other business in De Kalb. She wondered what had happened to her brother, Billy. He'd be twenty-seven now and everybody probably called him Bill and she didn't want to try to picture what he'd look like. The last time she had seen him he was a gangling, bashful kid of sixteen. Maybe he was married now and had a home of his own.

She sat on the back steps in the early afternoon sun and patted the head of a dog which had come barking up a few minutes after the taxi had hurried away, having been out in the fields somewhere or down at the barn. It was a fine collie but nothing like the setter they used to have.

Virginia sat there for what seemed hours, thinking they were never coming back, reviewing what she was going to say when they did, wondering if they could have gone for the day but knowing one cannot just get up and leave a farm with all the chores there are to do, when at last a new car turned in at the driveway. Her first thought was to hide and view these people from a distance before she showed herself, just to make sure they were her parents and avoid embarrassment if they were not, but she forced herself to sit there and watch the shiny car slide to a stop in the yard. She was relieved when she saw the familiar figures step from the car and she was surprised to see how little they had aged in the last eleven years, her father still a large, ungainly man with a face that looked as if it would break out into a smile (it always did), her mother a small woman with hair that had been white for as long as Virginia could remember, both with a few more wrinkles perhaps, but still very much alive.

When the happy reunion was over and they had gone into the house, her mother, flushed and excited, talking happily, and her father beaming (bless them both) she made them come out to the kitchen and sit while she told them something, overriding the protests of her father that he had a few little things he just ought to do before he sat down, and unable to stop her mother from starting tea.

Finally, impressed by her insistence, they did sit, a cloud of uncertainty hovering over their faces, while she tried to tell them what had happened to her.

"I just don't understand," her mother said at one point, and Virginia had to go back and tell it all over again.

"You mean you don't remember *anything?*" her father asked, incredulous.

She told them again firmly just how it was, how it felt to go to sleep in a hospital in Chicago one day and wake up in a motel in Los Angeles the next day eleven years later, how she felt when she walked out of the motel to find she was in a city she had never seen before.

"You poor child," her mother said, and her father shook his head uncomprehendingly.

"I've had enough training to know it's some form of amnesia," Virginia said. "But I'm not frightened by it because I know where I am now and who I am, which is important, and I don't want either of you to lose your heads about this."

"You mean it would've been different if you'd forgotten everything," Appleby said. "That'd have been serious."

"Exactly."

"But isn't this serious, Virginia?"

"It may be, Mom, but as long as I remember as much as I do I'm not too worried."

"What are you going to do?" Mrs. Appleby asked concernedly, not hearing the whistling teakettle.

"I don't know exactly." Then she said, "One thing you can be thankful for is that you don't have to tell me I'm married. I know I'm Mrs. Morley Don Fisher. I know what my husband looks like and where he lives and I'll go to him when I get used to the idea. I want to see if I feel the same way about him as I must have before. What I'd really like to know is what happened between the hospital and the motel."

Her father and mother, who had been exchanging startled glances, now looked away and Virginia knew something was wrong and her anxiety came back strong, a ball in her stomach, her mouth suddenly dry.

"What is it?" she asked. "What did I say?"

"Virginia," her mother then said softly, "you are not Mrs. Morley Don Fisher."

"We—we never heard of anybody named Fisher," her father said, shaking his head sadly.

"Never heard of him?" Virginia asked, her voice rising.

She had been so sure she had it all worked out. Now she could only stare at the two of them.

"You *are* married, however," her mother said. "You're Mrs. Walter Sherwood. Walter Evan Sherwood."

"He's a doctor," her father said. "Specializes in nerves."

"But how—?"

The three sat in a vacuum of silence avoiding each other's eyes, and the teakettle's shriek finally aroused Mrs. Appleby who was glad for an excuse to break the spell and do something.

"Homer," she said as she busied herself with the tea, "why don't you get that picture? The one on the dresser."

"Say, I forgot about that," he said rising. "It's a picture of you two, you and Walter," he told Virginia.

"We think Walter is wonderful," her mother said warmly, "what little we've ever got to see of him. He's a very busy man."

"When did I marry this…this Walter Sherwood?"

"In nineteen fifty-one. In Chicago."

"Here's the picture," her father said, coming back with the photograph folder.

"You and Walter didn't want to have your picture taken," Mrs. Appleby said. "Everybody does, you said, and you wanted to be different. But your father and I insisted."

Virginia opened the photograph and saw herself and the man she had seen in the motel, side by side, looking very happy.

"Why"—she swallowed hard—"that's him. That's Mr. Fisher."

"But it can't be, dear," her mother told her. "That's Dr. Sherwood."

Virginia examined his picture more closely, took in the honest bright eyes, the fine cut of face, the intelligent look. There could be no mistake in spite of the fact she had seen him only once and then only briefly.

"But why would he call himself Fisher? He had a driver's license and—well, so have I." She produced it from her bag and" showed it to them. "It's an accurate description of me and his must have been true of him, too."

"Why, I just don't know," her mother said, puzzled.

"It just don't make any sense at all," Appleby said in an irritated voice. "What were you two doing in California with changed names anyway?"

"You didn't write that you and Walter were going anywhere. We thought you were still in Michigan."

"Michigan?" Virginia shook her head in weary perplexity. "It gets more and more confusing."

They had tea now and sat around the kitchen table sipping it and nibbling on cookies Mrs. Appleby placed on the centerpiece.

"Maybe I'd better go back to where you've forgotten," her mother said. "You were operated on and the surgery came along well. The school let us know and we went to Chicago right away and saw you in the hospital there that night. You were going to school then, remember?"

"Yes, I remember. I was specializing in bacteriology."

"The old separator curiosity still at work," her father said, chuckling, "only on a more advanced scale."

"Your grades were good, so they let you take your final tests in June before summer school opened. Then you came home for the summer." Mrs. Appleby looked at her husband. "Did Virginia come home the next summer? I don't seem to remember."

"Let's see." Appleby frowned. "It was the summer of nineteen forty-eight she stayed in Chicago, so she was here the next summer."

"I'm glad I came home to help out, Dad."

"You were always a help," he said gruffly. "You'd get out in the oat field on days so hot I could hardly stand it. Made me feel almost ashamed of myself, you did."

"It was after you graduated in nineteen forty-seven that you got the job at Wright Memorial Hospital," Mrs. Appleby went on. "You were pretty happy there. You were head bacteriologist when you felt there three years later. They were sorry to lose you, they said."

"That's when I got married?"

Mrs. Appleby nodded. "We had a hard time getting your husband-to-be to take a minute off for it. I never saw such a busy man. He just wanted a short, civil ceremony."

"Funny man, Walter," her father said. "You talk to him and he seems like he's listening, but his mind's a million miles away. He's always thinking about something else."

"Oh, he isn't offensive about it," Mrs. Appleby hurried to explain. "He just has so much on his mind. He used to talk to us and tell us what he was doing, but we could never understand it. You could, though. You worshipped him, Virginia."

"I did?" Virginia asked, not conversant with this side of her nature.

"He was your kind of man," her father said. "Found a man who could answer all your questions for you."

"And I didn't know who he was," Virginia said morosely. "I woke up and there he was, all dressed up and ready to go somewhere and I didn't even know who he was. And to think I walked out on him."

Appleby took the last cookie. "I wouldn't feel too bad about it," he said gently. "You'll be hearing from him."

"Sure you will," her mother said comfortingly.

"I wonder." It had been from Wednesday to Monday, time for him to have called her parents. Why hadn't he done it? Surely a man missing a wife would have tried to get in touch with her parents by that time, wouldn't he? Or was that going to be another part of the mystery, the apparently never-to-be-solved puzzle that confronted her. "You say we went to Michigan?"

"It came suddenly," Mrs. Appleby said. "Near the end of fifty-one, wasn't it, Homer?"

Appleby nodded. "We were planning on a Chicago trip for Christmas, since you'd been out here the year before. But you wrote saying you both were going to Michigan."

"He found some kind of research work there he wanted. He never talked much about it."

"It was for the government," Appleby followed the last of the cookie with the remaining tea in his cup. "We were up there in fifty-three, weren't we, Mother? Nice little town, Merrittville. As clean a town as you'd find anywhere, right smack dab in the middle of the cherry country. Raise turkeys there, too."

"It's mostly resort country, Virginia. Sand and woods and lakes. Your father and Walter went fishing several times."

"Merrittville, Michigan. It's as if I never heard of it."

"You loved it. You had some sort of job that used your training, working for the same people as Walter. Only I don't think you worked all the time."

"No, that was the trouble." Appleby became uncomfortably conscious of his wife's glare.

"Trouble?" Virginia asked.

"No trouble," her mother reassured her. "Walter was just so tied up in his work we didn't get to see much of him, even when we were there. You were a little unhappy, you know how a person gets—moods? I've been guilty of it myself when I get so tired of having your father out there in the fields all day and doing the same thing over and over year in and year out. You just thought you weren't seeing enough of him, that's all. But a man has his work and no life is ideal. Even if it were, a person would find something to complain about."

"There were—we had no children?"

"No, Virginia. No children."

"He didn't have time, that Walter," Appleby said, chuckling.

"Homer!"

"Well," he grumbled, "I think he took everything too serious. Buried himself in his work. Why, if I worked on the farm the way he did with his work you'd never see me days on end."

"It's sometimes that way in science," Virginia said, seeking to rationalize the behavior of a husband she didn't even know. "I've known a lot of devoted people."

"There are some people who think science is going to replace religion."

"We're not going into that, Homer. You and Charlie Frank can argue about that. You always do." Charlie Frank was a neighbor much given to argument, mostly about the current farm program and price supports, but he could be lured into other avenues of disagreement.

"Where's Billy?" Virginia asked. "I half expected to find him working the farm when I arrived."

She saw her mother turn away, glanced at her father and saw his grim look, and before either said anything Virginia knew what had happened.

"He's—gone," Mrs. Appleby said. "Been gone nearly seven years."

"Little Billy?"

"He grew up fast, Virginia."

"He was a man in no time."

"How did it happen?"

"The war," her mother said simply, dabbing at her eyes with a handkerchief. "It took a lot of them, a lot more than we'd like to think and remember."

"But the war was over," Virginia said. "It was over a whole year before I had the operation, wasn't it?"

"Not the Korean War."

"Korean War?"

Her father explained that Billy Appleby had died in action just before Christmas in 1950. "Died like the man he was," he said somberly, "when the Chinese crossed the Yalu River."

"I didn't even know there had been another war," Virginia said softly. "Poor Billy."

And as her father told her about the war, its causes and its results, she fondled her remembrances of her brother and the times they had had together on the farm, and her anxiety was for the moment fully supplanted by the sorrow the fact of his death brought to her.

Later, when her father had gone out to do his chores she sat in the kitchen watching her mother at work, eased by the familiar sight of her bustling around the room and by the sounds she heard: the running of water in the sink the squeak of the floor when her mother walked over it (his grandfather hadn't put in enough nails when he built it, her father often complained), and the hum of the refrigerator. It was home and she couldn't get used to the idea that eleven years had passed since she'd been in it, at least in her memory of it.

Her mother talked about people she knew and people she didn't know, people who had children and people who had not, neighbors who had died and neighbors who were ill, and a few words of censure for this person or that words of praise for others who had shown unusual fortitude in living their plagued lives. But Virginia listened only halfheartedly, knowing that her mother was trying to draw her out of her situational preoccupation but not wanting to leave it.

Then, when it must have become obvious to her mother that what she was saying was not having its effect, Mrs. Appleby stopped at her side and said, "What are your plans, Virginia?"

"Plans?" Virginia shrugged. "I don't know. I thought everything would be settled once I arrived here, but I see nothing is settled at all. This is as far as I was able to see."

"Perhaps I could talk Homer into driving up to Merrittville. He likes it up there. We could get someone to watch the farm and do the chores."

"No. If I go to Merrittville I will go by myself."

"Do you think you should?"

"I got this far by myself. There's nothing really wrong with me. It's just as if I were twenty-two again. If I could travel when I was twenty-two I can travel now even though I can't remember what happened in between."

"But what about Dr. Sherwood?"

Virginia found nothing to reply to this. She knew what her mother meant: Suppose you find him a stranger? She had thought of that enough herself. There just was no answer.

"He's a neurophysiologist. Maybe he could do something about your condition."

"I don't understand why he hasn't got in touch with you," Virginia said heavily. "Maybe he thinks I'm angry or something. Maybe he thinks I've left him. Maybe we had an argument or something the night before. Things like that cause amnesia, you know."

"You would know more about things like that than I."

After the evening meal Virginia took the car into town and stopped at the library. There was something she had to know. She went to the reference room and took down the most recent volume of *Who's Who in America*. She found no notation of Morley Don Fisher. But she had no trouble at all in locating Walter Evan Sherwood. It read:

SHERWOOD, Walter Evan, neurophysiologist; b. Los Angeles, July 14, 1920; s. Evan Phillip and Gladys (Wray) S.; 3 yrs. Ill. Midwest Col., 1948; M.D., Ryerson Med. Sch. 1951; m. Virginia Appleby, 1951. Research fellow MacReynolds Found. 1951, consultant in neurophys. U.S. Dept. of Defense since 1952. Mem. Am. Physiol. Soc., Am. Neurol. Soc., Am. Electroencephalog, Soc. Home: 347 Walnut St., Merrittville, Mich.

When she finished the entry she closed the book, feeling a little more certain about things. The record was irrefutable. Dr. Sherwood lived in Merrittville, Michigan;

she was his wife and she ought to be there at 347 Walnut Street, whether he was or not.

It was as simple as that.

CHAPTER NINE

IT WAS JULY and the five hundred inhabitants of Merrittville were forced to share its two-block long business section with strangers, the thousands who lived brief lives in resorts and cottages on the numerous lakes in the area, and the never-to-be-acquainted-with faces of overnight visitors for" whom Merrittville was a mere stopping place, a point between points.

It was not only this increase in population that proved it was mid-summer. There was the Starlight drive-in theater, for example, a lonely, desolate waste of snow and speaker poles that stood like silent, starved sentinels in winter, now clean-swept and raked, its box office and its poles newly painted, its marquee alive with the next attraction. And then there were the three motels that each year closed their doors for winter after Labor Day but now closed them every day around three in the afternoon because that's when the "No Vacancy" signs went up.

Merrittville business was brisk, the fish were said to be biting everywhere (a rumor the resort men did not try to discourage), there was much to see and lots to do in this vacationland (map, anyone?) and tomorrow would be just as busy (where do they all come from?).

That is why, when Walter Sherwood drove into Merrittville, he was surprised to find it so bustling, having imagined it would be one of those sleepy little places one finds between larger towns, something like Webster, Illinois, and he realized now he need not have worried about it. It was so busy, in fact, that she found no parking space on Main Street, where he was going to stop and inquire for Walnut Street, so he kept on until be came to the drive-in, eyeing intersecting streets but seeing no signs. There was nothing beyond the drive-in, so he turned back and stopped at a service station at the edge of the business section where he asked after Walnut Street.

"Walnut Street?" the old, uniformed attendant repeated. "Why, that's just one street west of here. Can't miss it." And then, when he put up the hose and glanced at Sherwood, he squinted, ducked his head to spit a blob of tobacco on the concrete, and said, "Say, ain't you one of them guys from out at the clinic?"

"Clinic?"

"Yeah. You know, that place they built three miles west of town." And when Sherwood's face registered nothing, he added, "That Schlessenger place."

"You've got a good memory," Sherwood said noncommittally.

"Thought I spotted you. Never forget a face once it stops here. Yes, sir."

Sherwood drove the indicated block west and turned down the unmarked street, found 347 where he expected it to be, three and one-half blocks from Main, an old house little different from those around it, with white clapboard exterior that looked new, a two story house with gingerbread running along the roof line, a brick sidewalk extending from the street to the wide, open porch complete with swing. The ancient front door was wooden with a thick, beveled glass inset marked with curlicues.

He had started up the walk when an old man sitting on the porch of the house next door called to him.

"What you doing back in town, Doc?"

Sherwood stopped, did not know what to say to him. "Somebody said you quit out there." The man's chuckle drifted across the wide, sun-lighted swath of green. "Just goes to show you shouldn't believe all you hear. Ain't that right?"

Sherwood said only, "That's right," and hoped it would shut him up. It didn't.

"How's the Mrs.?"

He was tempted to say she broke her leg and he had to shoot her, because it was none of the old man's business, but he only replied, "Fine," and then as he continued up the walk he offered a silent prayer that she would be. Of course there was no basis for this wish, no more than there had been a reason for her to leave him at the motel. Why had she? Dr. Booey said she wasn't the kind of girl who'd run off, especially if she thought she was needed, and John Trankle, the Loop physician who had known her and supplied the picture of her that proved she was the girl in the motel (it had bothered Sherwood a little that he had kept it), had only fine things to say about her, what a good student she was, how helpful she had been in school, particularly to him, and how he had asked her to marry him once but she had just laughed at him. That part of it rankled Sherwood the most and he was not immediately aware why. How could you feel possession for a wife you had never known, a woman you had seen but once and then only briefly and under trying circumstances?

He had half expected to find her there in Merrittville at the house ahead of time, but the old man next door had spoiled that. He wouldn't have asked about her if he had seen her go in.

He tried several keys before he found the one that fitted the lock, let himself into the cool interior. As he moved from the small hall to the living room he noticed the musty smell that houses get that are closed in the summer, and it stayed with him as he toured the downstairs and upstairs (he tried not to pay too much attention to her things, this woman who had shared six years of his unremembered life), found the house to be much as he had expected from the outside, very old, ornate, but comfortable and brightly decorated. He wondered: Am I renting this or do I own it? And he chuckled at the absurdity of a man's not knowing a thing like that.

So far, so good, he thought. A rallying point. I've come a long way for a man with amnesia. From Los Angeles, to be exact. I've found I've gone to Midwest College, Ryerson Medical School, knew a man there by the name of Dr. Booey (what the devil's his first name?), and I was an eager beaver who got excellent grades and took a job at Schlessenger Institute in Merrittville, Michigan. I'm married to a girl named Virginia, and we live in this house.

What next? What part shall I unravel now?

The Institute.

Andrew Schlessenger is the name, according to Dr. Booey. Dr. Andrew Schlessenger.

Maybe Virginia would be there.

He nearly missed Schlessenger Institute on his swing west of town, thinking the modern building he passed on his right was a motel or resort, but the sign on the lawn registered on his brain after he had turned away to look for it farther on. The sign said Schlessenger Institute.

So he found a side road, turned around and drove back slowly, taking in the contemporary structure built of ledge-rock and brick and wood with an overhanging roof, a long, low building that hugged the ground and had none of the severity he had expected. The road was slightly higher and Sherwood could look over it enough to see it was deeper than he had thought, the wing of the L extending far to the rear.

He turned into the cement drive and parked with three other cars to one side of the entrance and went in. At once he was in a small, elegantly furnished, thickly carpeted waiting room that would have done justice to a stock brokerage office. His presence must have registered somewhere because a woman opened one of the thick paneled doors and looked at him questioningly.

At at once her face brightened.

"Why, Dr. Sherwood!" A thin woman in her thirties wearing a trim business suit with a lapel watch, she came toward him, extending a hand, smiling, and he could see she was genuinely pleased to see him. "I never expected to see you…"

"You might say that goes both ways." He took the hand. It was soft and cool.

"You ought to let people know when you're coming, Doctor. You gave me quite a start." She turned her head slightly as if remembering there was someone behind her. "Dr. Schlessenger will certainly be surprised to see you."

"He's here then?"

"Of course. Where did you think he'd be?" She laughed a little and her eyes were without guile and they stood there awkwardly, the woman radiating friendliness and waiting for him to say something and Sherwood wanting to go directly to the doctor's office but not wanting to ask the way.

"Maybe you'd better be the advance guard," he suggested brilliantly. "Don't want to surprise him, too."

"Oh, he'll be surprised either way." She turned and he stepped to her side as she walked toward the door she had come through. "We were all disturbed when you stepped out like that."

"I'm sorry," he said.

They were through the door now into a small inner office, obviously the woman's. She stopped before another door and knocked.

"Yes?" from the inside.

She opened the door. Over her shoulder Sherwood could see a ruddy face, a neat blond mustache, athlete's shoulders, slicked back thin blond hair and bright blue eyes, all belonging to a man who sat at a massive desk.

"Dr. Sherwood's come back," she said simply, stepping aside for him to see.

"Sherwood?" The man twisted a little in the swivel chair to get a better look at him across the room and said, "It *is* Sherwood! What the devil are you doing here?" He left the chair and came across the carpeted floor in slow, easy strides, extending a large hand that Sherwood, in shaking it, found strong. "So you've decided to come back!"

"Believe it or not," the woman said, "he just walked in." She closed the door behind her as she went out.

Schlessenger guided him to a leather chair beside the desk, saying gruffly, "Sit down, Doctor," and taking the swivel chair behind the desk. "You might have let us know you were coming."

"I didn't know what kind of reception I'd get," Sherwood said, shooting in the dark. Schlessenger was a

few years older than he, the other side of forty. Good
looking. Distinguished looking, actually.

"Schlessenger Institute is human," Schlessenger said.
"As such it allows for human failings in its employees. I
am least tolerant of myself, as any of them can tell you, and
as you already know." He coughed a little, as if trying to
emphasize this point. "You may be in charge of a research
organization someday, my boy. Then you'll know the
headache it really is. What brings you back to Merrittville?
Ready to go back to work?"

"Just following a thread, Doctor."

"A thread, eh? Well, you left plenty of them dangling
here when you quit, Walter. Men like you aren't easily
replaced." There was no question of the admonition in his
voice. He went on dryly, "But don't get the idea I've been
hurt. No Schlessenger Institute Research Fellow is
indispensable." He gave a short, humorless laugh.
"Except me, of course."

Schlessenger sighed, rose from the swivel chair and
moved to a cabinet at the side of the room, throwing open
the doors that revealed a well-stocked liquor supply, saying,
"I suppose you've found things difficult on your own, eh?
Research fellows need good direction." When Sherwood
did not answer, he said, "My guess is you're wondering if
your position has been filled. Well, it isn't. I thought
you'd be back for it."

Returning from the cabinet, he handed Sherwood a
drink and said, "For your information, nothing has
changed. Black is still fathering his parasites, Rayburn has
been breeding more resistant mice strains every day and
sending them into the wild blue yonder each new crop, and
Cox, Wilhelm and Heneberry are still occupied. Of course
all of this shouldn't be news to you, but don't press me for

details. You know it's not my policy to discuss the work of one man with another."

Sherwood tasted the drink. It was good scotch. He knew by Schlessenger's immaculate appearance and the plush office that it would be good scotch. But why didn't the man stop talking? He wanted to shout: Why don't you shut up or say something that means something? I had counted on your bringing something back to me and now you're pushing it farther away than ever.

"Do you, Walter?" Schlessenger was saying.

"Do I what?"

"Do you want to come back?"

Sherwood moved, uncomfortable in the leather chair, knowing he would have to go through all the questions again and not relishing the prospect. Well, where to begin?

Schlessenger said, "Something bothering you?"

Sherwood nodded. "To put it bluntly, yes." He smiled wryly. "I never saw you before in my life."

Schlessenger's features went slack, the chair came forward, the doctor put his drink on the polished desktop and looked across at him concernedly. "What did you say?"

"I said I don't recall ever seeing you, I don't know you and I don't know what you're talking about."

Schlessenger sucked in his breath. "Whatever's wrong with you, Walter?"

"I just told you. I don't remember anything."

"But you *must* remember!"

Sherwood shook his head. "I don't recall anything of the last eleven years. I've been retracing my steps, following a thread, as I said, and the thread has brought me here. What can you tell me about Walter Sherwood,

Doctor Schlessenger? All I know is I came to work here in nineteen fifty-one. That's all. What happened after that?"

Schlessenger stared.

They all stared, didn't they? Trefethen, Booey, Trankle...and now Schlessenger.

"Walter," Schlessenger said in a choked voice, "I—" Then his face hardened, and he said sharply, "Walter, I have no time for practical jokes."

"Neither have I, Doctor."

"But eleven years—Walter, it's unbelievable!"

"It is nevertheless true. It so happens I woke up in Los Angeles on July eleventh and I don't remember anything before that back to May fifteenth, nineteen forty-six. There you have it."

Schlessenger looked startled. "July eleventh? Why, that was only last week."

"I've lived five years in the past week."

"But—" Schlessenger's face was blanched and he seemed to have difficulty going on. Then he said, "Walter, on July tenth you were at the Coronado Motel. You spent the night there. Do you mean to tell me—"

"You know about that?"

"Of course I do. We all stayed at the motel. Don't you remember? You, your wife and I. We were going to the convention in Santa Barbara. Do you mean to tell me you really don't remember?"

CHAPTER TEN

SHERWOOD SAID SHARPLY, "I said I don't remember."

"Of course you did, but—" Schlessenger gave him a look that appealed to him to end this nonsense. "Walter, I—"

"What about the motel?" Sherwood prodded relentlessly. Schlessenger let out his breath in a big sigh. "I was in the next cabin and..." He shook his head. "This is ridiculous."

"The convention. You said something about a convention."

"I went to the convention. You never made it."

"Why?"

Schlessenger frowned, rose with his drink, started to walk the floor slowly, in a study, choosing his words carefully. "Walter, I've had twenty some odd years of schooling, I've waded through thousands of books, have been counseled by hundreds of learned men and lately I've run a research organization. But never, never have I run across anything as bizarre as this thing you tell me. While amnesia isn't my province, I pride myself on how much I've been able to absorb from other fields, including psychiatry, and I want you to know yours an truly an unusual case. What makes it almost unbelievable is that you—well, you were so close to the Institute and to me, and now"—he turned to Sherwood—"you sit there a complete stranger."

"Why didn't I make it to the convention?"

Schlessenger shrugged. "I don't know. I wish I did. I wish I could tell you." He returned to the desk. "I'll tell you what I can. Maybe it would help, if you really don't remember." He sat in the chair, put his drink on the desk, his elbows on the desktop, fingers touching before his face, his eyes focussing on the opposite wall. "We went out together in your car. You, your wife and I. We made it a leisurely trip out, even stopping at the Grand Canyon because Mrs. Sherwood had never seen it."

Schlessenger turned to him. "You were unusually quiet, Walter, and—well, a little jumpy. I remember being rather concerned about it. Maybe what was going to happen was getting ready to happen even then, but perhaps I should have done something about it, but I had my mind on other things—the convention, mostly.

"When we reached Los Angeles you suggested we stop in Eagle Rock. You said you used to live there. I had no objection. We could have reached Santa Barbara that night, but there would have been no particular point in doing so. We stayed at the Coronado, you and Ginny in one cabin and I in the next. I had no inkling of what was going to happen."

"What did happen?"

"You woke me up at about two in the morning. I went to the door and there you stood looking, I should say, a little wild-eyed. I'll admit I was a little surly. I'd been awakened from a sound sleep and I thought you and Ginny had been out carousing around. Of course I should have known better. I did, as soon as I saw you were in your robe and perfectly sober. I invited you in and asked you what was the trouble. You sat down and told me you were quitting. Just like that. You said you were getting out of research entirely.

"Of course I was shocked. I asked you why and you said you'd been thinking about it ever since you came to the Institute and had finally decided that night to have done with it. I tried to argue you out of it, but you were immovable. I urged you to think it over, take a leave of absence if necessary, but you said you'd made your decision and you were through right then and there."

"Did I give any reason?"

Schlessenger shook his head gravely. "I tried to get you to talk sense, but you were so wrought up you were incapable of it. I asked you if your wife concurred in the decision and you said she did, but I wasn't satisfied until you brought Mrs. Sherwood over. She was, if anything, more upset about the whole thing than you were. But she said it was your decision to make and if that's the way you felt about it she wasn't going to try to change you. She was obviously worried to death about you, just as I was. Why you waited until we reached Los Angeles to tell us such a thing I'll never understand."

"You accepted the resignation then?"

"What else could I do? I learned long ago you can't get work out of people who have their minds and hearts on something else. Oh, we sat around arguing about it and there was a little name-calling, but there was no changing your mind."

"Didn't you try to see us in the morning?"

"To be frank," Schlessenger said, "the longer I thought about it the angrier I got. I slept very little the rest of the night and when morning came I ignored you completely, rented a car and drove the rest of the way to Santa Barbara. When you stepped out through the door after you told me you quit, you were through, I decided. I've always believed in a clean break, once it's been made. No recriminations, no apologies. You said—that's the way you wanted it; that's the way I let you have it."

"I see." Now the thread was complete. From Eagle Rock to Midwest to Ryerson to Merrittville and back to Eagle Rock. And it all added up to nothing really helpful. Sherwood had thought that perhaps knowing all that had preceded the blanking out, his memory would come back in a rush. But the blank spaces were just as empty as before, filled in only by what he'd learned from others, and not one thing had triggered the expected rush of recall. There wasn't even the beginning of a recollection.

Schlessenger had been watching him and said now in a large voice, "Don't look so downcast, Walter. It is my professional opinion that this amnesia of yours won't last forever."

Sherwood said morosely, "I wish I could be sure of that."

"Be sure of it because I am. It's obvious your wrought-up state was responsible. Armed with that knowledge, any psychiatrist ought to break down the barrier to the unremembered time. It's done every day."

"I don't think it will be that easy."

Schlessenger said sharply, "Don't contradict me. I don't like it. It so happens I know what I'm talking about, my boy. I'm telling you progress can be made in such conditions as yours. That business out in Los Angeles was the straw that broke the camel's back, to employ a cliche. The rubber band tightens and grows thin as it stretches, but it can't be stretched too far or it will break. That's what has happened to you, Walter. Amnesia's not fatal. It's merely the symptoms of some deeper trouble. You need treatment and my advice is not to delay it. There are some good men in Detroit."

"I thought coming here to Merrittville might be better than treatment. But it has done nothing."

"Of course it hasn't. You need expert help. It's nothing you can do by yourself, believe me. I'm sure your wife would agree with me. By the way, where is Mrs. Sherwood?"

"I haven't seen her."

"Haven't seen her?"

"Not since all this started."

"Has she left you?"

"Yes." There was no need to go into it.

"I never thought she'd be capable of a thing like that." His eyes were dark in reproach. "I thought she was a fine woman. What a time to desert you! Just when you need her most. Do you have any idea where she is?"

"I'm afraid not. I thought she might have come back to Merrittville."

"She didn't even tell you where she was going? I'd say that was unpardonably cruel of her."

The door Sherwood had come through suddenly opened and both men turned to stare at the woman who stood there.

"Oh!" she said. "I—I didn't know—Miss Lawson wasn't out here and—"

"Where's that woman," Schlessenger said, rising.

"Sorry, Andrew," the woman said, then she nodded to Sherwood and said, "Doctor."

Sherwood nodded in return. There was something odd about this woman and the way their glances locked for a moment. She only looked away when Schlessenger said, "Georgia, Dr. Sherwood and I—"

"I see," she said apologetically. "I shouldn't have come barging in." She backed through the door and closed it, her eyes trying desperately to keep from Sherwood's.

"My wife," Schlessenger said, nodding toward the door and sighing. "You're supposed to know her, so introductions would have sounded strange to her and I'd have to explain...and I don't know how you feel about everybody knowing..." His voice trailed off.

"It's all right," Sherwood said, suddenly sharing Schlessenger's embarrassment and not knowing why.

"Would you like to see your laboratory?" Schlessenger asked suddenly. "Perhaps it would help bring something back."

"Yes, I'd like to do that," Sherwood said, rising with him, "but I suppose it will be like everything else—completely strange."

"It will be if you're convinced of it." Schlessenger led him through a door. "You've got to think in terms of your memory coming back or it never will. It's always like this, first total inability to recall, then a glimmer here, a glimmer there, and finally a rush of remembering that brings everything back."

They walked down a bright, wide hallway, passing doors labeled Dr. Anthony Black, Dr. Robert Rayburn, Dr. Herman Wilhelm, and others, all in gold letters on polished brass doorknobs, thick, heavy doors, until they came to the one labeled Dr. Walter E. Sherwood. Schlessenger inserted a silver key, opened the door and clicked on the lights, though there was no need for them with all the daylight coming through the windows at the top of the far wall.

"Well, here you are," Schlessenger said. "Remember it at all?"

Both men were silent as they stood there, Sherwood seeing the gleaming instruments, the fine array of apparatus, all of it strange to him, conscious of Schlessenger's eyes on him, feeling all the while as if he were standing in someone's grave, still knowing his hands were the hands that must have moved that beaker there, that had set the knurled knobs of that machine over there, whatever it was, a place of study for a studious stranger, the stranger that was Walter Evan Sherwood a month ago, a year ago, and more.

"Well?" Schlessenger asked hopefully.

"Nothing," Sherwood said huskily. "I'm afraid it does nothing. I wouldn't know where to begin in a place like this."

"That's too bad, Walter, it really is."

"What did I do here?"

"I have a large grant from the National Science Foundation to carryon lines of research that appear to be important to me," Schlessenger explained. "I selected you from among many because I had heard about your work, read some of your articles. You were an individualist and that's what I wanted, a man with imagination and daring. You didn't care much for established fact or rules or precedent. You had directness and inspiration."

Schlessenger's voice boomed from the walls as if in eulogy for the man whose tomb this was, this clutter of machines and instruments the mementos in the shrine, even to the notes in his own hand Sherwood saw on a long bench.

"I never regretted for a minute that you came to work for me," Schlessenger said. "I gave you a free hand."

"What kind of work was I doing?"

Schlessenger shrugged. "Oh, you had a lot of irons in the fire. I don't know just which of your various projects you were concerned with at the moment you left."

"I had more than one thing going, then?"

"When you tired of one you'd go on to the next."

"Didn't I have a main project, a number one interest?"

The doctor eyed him without expression. "Yes, but it's quite involved, Walter, and in your present condition, I..."

"I'll try to understand."

"You wouldn't, Walter."

Sherwood grinned. "Then there'd be no harm in telling me, would there?"

"Well..." Schlessenger flushed. "You've forgotten your schooling, it's stupid to try, but if you insist..." He sat on one of the benches. "Over there" he said, pointing to one section of the room where a long machine that looked like a radio control panel covered half the wall with a window above it looking into another room, "is an electroencephalograph. Next to it is a toposcope, that device with that cluster of cathode ray tubes in the form of the cranium as seen from above. You were working with both of those, stimulating the cortex, the sensorimotor strip, the various gyri. In that area you were evaluating the efficacy of the electronic stroboscope in producing desirable paroxysmal cerebral dysrhythmia. Follow me?"

"No," Sherwood said, feeling an anger starting because Schlessenger had deliberately cloaked his remarks in technical language. "I don't understand it at all."

"Well, I said you wouldn't, remember?"

"You could have put it a hell of a lot more simply, if you ask me."

"I could have," Schlessenger said tartly, "but I don't see why I should." Then he said, "It will all be coming back to you soon enough."

"You think so?"

"Certainly," Schlessenger said, walking to the door. "Shall we go?"

"I suppose," Sherwood said, joining him and taking one last look around. He saw a safe in a corner, a thing he hadn't noticed before, and was on the point of asking the doctor about it when Schlessenger pulled the door shut saying, "I'd introduce you to the others except that they are all at work." They were going back down the hall the way they had come. "They're working on problems and it's best not to disturb them when they are. I'd suggest your not meeting any of them anyway in your condition."

When they entered the office again Schlessenger said, "Yours is definitely a case of classical amnesia, Walter, and I want to see you undergoing treatment as quickly as possible. You can't come back here the way you are."

Sherwood leaned on the leather chair facing Schlessenger, who had taken the chair behind the desk again. "I just thought of something, Doctor."

"What is it?"

"Morley Don Fisher. I have a driver's license made out in that name with all my pertinent statistics. It seems I live in a nonexistent place in Webster, Illinois."

"I suppose that would puzzle you. But it was just a matter of security precaution, that's all."

"Security precaution? Why?"

"I always insist on an alternate identity when away from the Institute."

"I don't understand."

"Obviously," Schlessenger said dryly.   "It's like everything else."

"But there are no guards around here, no security precautions that I can see. Why should a thing like that be necessary? Was my work of such a secret nature?"

Schlessenger opened a tray on the desk, offered Sherwood a cigarette, took one himself, lit Sherwood's and, with the lighter in his right hand, paused before he spun the wheel, gazing at Sherwood, drawing on his cigarette.

"I don't know what I should tell you, since you are no longer apprised of what goes on here, but—" and he paused to spark the lighter "—I have a dozen memoranda from the Department of Defense and several government agencies down the line suggesting such security precautions and offering assistance in cases where it is needed." He inhaled deeply, blew out a plume of smoke.

"Obviously you thought they were needed."

"I assumed a different identity myself, Walter."

"You still haven't said why."

"Up here at Merrittville," Schlessenger said patiently, "a stranger stands out like a red flag—at least most of the year he does. So there is no need for much security safeguard here, at least anything elaborate. But out on the road it's a different story. Perhaps you don't know there is still a well-organized espionage system in this country and anything we can do to prevent incidents or mishaps, including outright kidnapping, is worth trying. You have read, no doubt, about scientists who supposedly fled to other countries, carrying their own country's secrets with them."

"What you are saying then is that what I was doing was vital to the, defense of the United States?"

"What work isn't? Farming, manufacturing, medicine—name anything. But farming and most manufacturing and medicine aren't done on grants from the National Science Foundation. That way you come close to defense."

Sherwood shook his head. "I still don't see why."

"Why shouldn't I try to do everything I can for you?" the doctor said with less grace than usual. "You're being rather unkind, I'd say, for the protection I arranged for." Then he softened. "Walter, it's just the way things are done nowadays. You've been out of touch for eleven years. Why, the government itself insisted on a thorough check on you before I was allowed to touch you. Now do you understand?"

"Frankly, no."

Schlessenger stiffened, said coolly, "Would you like to see a few directives on that very subject?"

"Never mind."

"I'm not sure I appreciate the curious tack your mind has taken, Walter. We've had our differences, but mostly along lines of procedure, never on loyalty or motives." He looked at his curved wristwatch. "I'm sorry, but I have an appointment, Walter. He's probably waiting in the outer office right now." As he moved Sherwood to the door, he said, "I'll give some thought to your affliction. I know a dozen good men in the field. You keep in touch, do you hear?"

"Yes," Sherwood said without feeling. To his surprise there was someone waiting in the outer office.

The air outside was bracing and balmy and not unlike California air and the sun in the sky, he decided, looked no different from what it did in Los Angeles, or Chicago, or the Pacific, which was a good thing to know because no matter how unkind time would be to him there would always be basic things like sun, air and earth, though the people would change and be older, and so would he, until he could grow older no more but cease to enjoy these things, and he thought: Why the worry? Why am I pursuing this thing? Why don't I just take things for what they are and start my life over again and forget trying to tie those loose thread-ends together?

He went to the car, a study of a man, deep in thought, head down, frowning. He reached for the door handle and looked up into bright brown eyes.

It was Georgia. Mrs. Schlessenger. She was standing by the car door and now that she saw him she turned to look furtively back at the entrance. She was a head shorter than he, a woman in a gray skirt and white sweater, fine-boned and youthful-looking, freckled and intense now as she looked at him again with urgency in her eyes.

"I'm sorry," Sherwood said. "I didn't see you."

She said nothing, but Sherwood could see the white knuckles of the hand that clutched the side of the car. Seeing him look at it, she self-consciously removed the hand and it left a moist imprint, and her hands had difficulty settling themselves, twisting and turning, until she forced them to her sides where they remained clenched.

"Did you want to say something?" Sherwood asked.

In answer, the woman's mouth moved as if she would, indeed, like to say something but could not find the strength to do so. Then her eyes welled with tears, she moaned softly, leaned her head against an arm she had flung up on the side of the car.

He touched her shoulder.

She winced, turned and stepped away, and when he started toward her, she said, "No, please!" and she made long strides toward the building.

He stared after her.

Sherwood was still puzzled when he opened the door at 347 Walnut Street, went through the little hallway, and entered the living room to find his wife sitting there waiting for him.

"Hello," Virginia said.

CHAPTER ELEVEN

SHERWOOD stood at the door and Virginia sat in the rocker facing him, and they were silent and awkward with immobility. Sherwood thought: she's lovely.

The moment stretched out so long they both flushed with the embarrassment of it and their mute examination of each other. Finally he said lamely, "Hello," and tried to put something of how he felt in the greeting, but when he heard the word it sounded empty and told nothing about his racing heart and his joy in seeing her at last.

She smiled and the room seemed brighter for it, and she said, "I heard you on the steps and at the door and knew you were coming. Perhaps I shouldn't have surprised you like this. It wasn't fair."

Now Sherwood's mind was out-racing his heart and he wanted to question her, tell her what was wrong, hear from her the truth of things, yet he didn't want her to know his complete strangeness yet. From the look of her it seemed she did not hold his running out on her against him, which was good. He said, "I've just come from the Institute," trusting that to be casual and ordinary. He added, "I'm glad you're here," and managed a smile.

Her eyes flickered to her hands, but she forced them up to meet his, bright and determined, and they both laughed a little and the awkwardness lifted slightly.

"How are things out there?" she asked.

"All right."

The awkwardness rushed in again and they found themselves looking uncertainly at each other, waiting for the next move in the game, Sherwood feeling the sweat on his forehead and thinking *have I botched this, does she know, has she guessed?*

Something resolute settled on Virginia's face and she rose from the rocker. He found her young and sturdy looking and a head shorter than he. He watched as she put a fine-boned hand on the knob of the old rocker and said, "I suppose you are wondering why I left the motel before you returned." She did not look at him.

"Please sit down," he said. He watched her, a pale Virginia now, as she sank back to the chair, and he wondered if she was beginning to be frightened of him. "There is something I have to tell you, something important." He reached for a straight-backed chair, dragged it across the floor and set it a few feet away facing her. He sat on the edge of the chair and leaned toward her. "It will probably shock you."

"Will it?" Her voice was a little shrill, and she knew he was going to tell her about her amnesia, something grave, tell her how long it would be before she would remember him...

"Yes." He struggled to find the proper words, then said, "The first time I recall seeing you is back in the motel in Los Angeles a week ago. Everything before that is blank for eleven years. I seem to have amnesia."

He saw wonderment grow in her eyes, saw the pupils widen in surprise, the face blanch further, and he thought this *is* a shock to her, will she be able to stand it?

"You?" she said, her lips barely moving. "*You* have amnesia?" He could barely hear her.

"Yes." He hoped she'd understand, hoped she'd be willing to serve as his memory until he found his again. It would be no easy task, being depended upon for remembering, and unless she went into it whole-heartedly, with complete understanding and without aversion to the mental aberration it was, there would be no sense in trying it. He had to know that before anything else.

"But—I" She stopped, her mouth open a little, her eyes staring uncomprehendingly.

Sherwood thought: It's too much for her.

Then he said, "It's not as if I were ready for the booby hatch or something, it's just that I don't remember, that's all. Otherwise I'm perfectly normal. It's nothing to be frightened of."

She swallowed. "I—I'm not frightened. It's just that—" He waited and watched her struggle for words.

Finally she put her lips together and said evenly, "It so happens that I don't remember either."

Now Sherwood stared, clutched the side of the chair at the seat and said hoarsely, "What?"

"I don't remember either," she repeated, tears welling in her eyes. "I woke up in the motel and you were standing there and I didn't know who in the world you were. Then I went outside and I didn't know what town it was, I'd never been there before, and when I found out it was Los Angeles, I thought I'd gone crazy."

"So it's happened to you, too," Sherwood said softly, numbly.

"Yes," she said, finding a handkerchief in her purse and dabbing at her eyes. "I thought I was Mrs. Fisher, that I had suddenly come down with amnesia. I was frightened, took some of your money and ran home, hoping it would all end and the memories would come flooding back. But they never did." She looked at him bleakly. "That's where I found out who I really am, there at home, and I learned you were a neurophysiologist and I thought when I came here you'd know what to do and all my troubles would be over." She paused and then said. "Now I find they're not over at all."

Sherwood sat chilled by what she had said. A few minutes ago he felt he had at last reached the end of his search, the vistas of the missing years just beyond Virginia's eyes, the clouds hovering over the view to be blown away by her account of everything that had occurred, even the little things. Now he knew she had felt the same thing about him, and there would be no revelation, no recounting, no remembrance of things past.

The blind leading the blind.

"And you thought I—" She stopped.

"Yes."

Then his chair was at hers, their knees nearly touching, and they talked hard and earnestly, drawn by the common enigma, each ferreting out scraps of information from the other, trying to cover every move, every thought in the days since July eleventh, when the curtain had fallen over their minds, leaving them rudderless and adrift in a world grown older and in many ways strange. And in the talk, faintly felt at first, was strength, a bond, a kinship, a mutual accord the equally infirm feel, each for the other, and the strength grew as they talked the unminded minutes away until the room darkened with the late afternoon.

When the heat of exchange was over, they sat in the gathering dusk, dazed and exhausted, and Sherwood took her hand, which was on the arm of the rocker, and held it.

From the rear of the house came a click, followed by the hum of the refrigerator, and Sherwood stirred and said, "You don't know this house any better than I do then."

"No. The clothes in the drawers and closets upstairs must be my clothes but I don't recall buying them."

"I thought the same way about the things I found."

"I knew I had the right house. The man next door shouted at me, said you'd been here and gone, but I rang the bell first just to make sure. Then I used one of the keys in my case. I came in and brought the mail with me, a statement from the bank, some bills, a few circulars. Nothing important. I went around the house trying to remember things, but it didn't work. I decided then to wait for you."

They were silent for a while still sensing the wonderment of it. Then Virginia said, "I never heard of two people getting amnesia at the same time."

"Neither did I."

"How could it happen?"

"I don't know. But even supposing that two people could get amnesia at the same time, it seems odd that a man and wife would suffer from it on the same day of the year."

"Perhaps not if they were subjected to the same trying experiences that would bring it on," Virginia said. "Of course they would have to have the same temperament, the same failings."

"But forgetting the same period of their lives so completely—forgetting back to the same day?" Sherwood shook his head. "No. There is more to it than that, Virginia."

"I'm sure there is. Your work, for example."

"I've thought of that. You say you saw your parents in De Kalb. What do they think happened?"

"They think this happened only to me. They're worried about it, of course, but they're sure you will be able to straighten things out."

"Did they mention anything about my work?"

"Only that you buried yourself in it."

"That's no help."

"No."

"I remember nothing of it. All I remember that might help is my days with the medics."

"Medics?"

"Army days."

"I didn't know you were in the army."

Sherwood stretched muscles cramped from sitting on the chair. "That's where it all started. That and my father." He shot a glance at her. "You're proof that I haven't gone off my rocker. I had my doubts for a while."

"What about your father?"

He said gruffly, "He died in a hospital for the insane while I was in the army."

"I'm sorry."

"He'd been getting worse for years. I hated leaving him at a time like that, but I had no choice. We were very close."

Virginia said nothing.

"Then in the army I saw the same thing happen to men who would have led perfectly normal lives if they hadn't

111

been pushed too far. That's when I began to get the idea about studying the brain, trying to find out why this should happen, see if there was any way to prevent it. I had the idea when I was discharged but I didn't know exactly how I was going to pursue it. Now I know what I did, though I can't remember it, of course. As I said, for a while I was afraid I'd pushed myself too far, that my mind had backtracked under the pressure. Now I know that's not true, now that you're here and it's happened to you, too."

"I'm different," Virginia said. "That swamped feeling is gone. No work, no classes, no studying. I feel much more free than I did then, though it seems only a week ago I was going to school and helping John Trankle with his cramming."

"We're older."

"We're grown."

"Inside."

She smiled. "We feel the effects though we don't know the cause."

"Two lost souls," he said dismally. Then he said harshly, "Why can't we remember? It's all in our heads, isn't it?"

"I wish I could tell you."

He said glumly, "Lost between sundown and sunup: eleven years."

"I wonder what kind of years they were, Walter. I would like very much to think they were happy years."

He eyed her steadily. "They were happy years."

"Thank you for thinking that."

"I'm sure of it." He got to his feet and stretched in the darkness, went to the window and looked out on the street. There were lights in the houses across the street but he made no move to turn on lights in the room. "Before you came, I was looking for the cause for this thing in my background. Just as everyone I talked to said, I thought it might have been that I pushed myself too hard, or there might have been some unpleasantness I wasn't willing to face up to. It was a question of finding where the string broke and finding the ends and tying them together."

"Now you don't think so?"

"No. Now that you're here and it's happened to you I can't think that way any more." He turned to her, saw her vaguely in the gloom. "It has something to do with the Institute and with my work there."

"You were just out there. What did they say?"

"Nothing. I talked with Schlessenger—Doctor Andrew Schlessenger runs the place, didn't I tell you? He wasn't any help."

"You mentioned him. What kind of work were you doing? Did he say?"

"He was vague. I worked with the brain all right, but he didn't seem to think my amnesia could be related to the work."

"Maybe you carried on a secret project, something you didn't tell him about."

"I doubt that. He'd know about it if anybody would."

"What kind of man is this Doctor Schlessenger?"

"I found him overbearing. He dresses well, has a fine office and a secretary who wears a lapel watch. You should see the building."

"New?"

"Very modern. Ranch style. I passed it the first time without knowing what it was. Looks like anything but a research institution. The laboratories are all modern, too. At least mine was."

"You saw yours?"

Sherwood nodded. "He showed me around."

"You said he wouldn't talk about your work?"

"He said I wouldn't understand it. I guess he's right."

"How many people work out there?"

"Half a dozen."

"I don't know whether I trust this Schlessenger."

"Why?"

"Intuition…was he sympathetic?"

"Yes, he was sympathetic. He thought I wanted my job back. Told me how I quit that night in the motel. He thinks I ought to have psychiatric treatment."

"I wonder why you wanted to quit the Institute."

"So do I." Sherwood returned to the window. The lights at the street corners were on now. "Schlessenger said he tried to get me to stay, but I was determined to quit and nothing would sway me. I wonder if I could talk with any of these other researchers they would know why."

"Why don't you?"

"Schlessenger suggested it would be better if I didn't."

"Why for heaven's sake?"

"My 'condition,' as he described it."

"I wouldn't let that stop me."

"Maybe you're right."

"I think I am," Virginia said cheerfully, "but I'm not going to be lured out of this house like this. I'm famished. Aren't you?"

"Yes." He turned, felt along the wall until he found a light switch and clicked it on. "What's for dinner?"

"I don't know. First, I'm going to take a bath. Then I want to see the kind of taste in a clothes my alter ego had."

"Do you suppose the people who lived here before ever had a drink before dinner?"

She laughed. "That will be worth investigating."

CHAPTER TWELVE

FROM where they stood in the darkness on the front porch of the Rayburn home, they could see through the nearly closed slats of the Venetian blinds into eerie blueness of the living room where the television set was a glowing, commanding presence. Sherwood pressed the button and they heard the harsh rasp of the buzzer over the door, and this broke the spell inside; there was movement, the porch light went on, and a long-faced man peered out at them through the opening door. In one movement he pushed open the screen, joined them on the porch and closed both doors behind him.

"Dr. Sherwood," the lean-faced man said in a low voice. He nodded gravely to Virginia and said, "Mrs. Sherwood," and then turned black eyes back to Sherwood.

There could be no question of the man's identity. They had the right address, Sherwood was sure of that, and he'd been called by name, so he said, "Dr. Rayburn, I—"

But Rayburn cut him off with a wave of his hand. "Before you say anything, Doctor, I want you to know I can be of no help."

Sherwood said dryly, "I haven't asked you for any yet." Rayburn was unperturbed. "Dr. Schlessenger said you'd be calling."

"That's funny. I didn't tell him I would be."

"He said you claim you are suffering from amnesia."

"It is a fact, Doctor."

"He also said you feel certain—ah, facts—might help you regain your memory."

Sherwood said equably, "Isn't that a logical assumption?"

"Perhaps so, but you know that any information has to clear through Dr. Schlessenger."

"No, I don't know. I have amnesia, remember?"

"It's true, Doctor," Virginia said.

"If it's true, all I can say is I'm sorry to hear it."

Dr. Rayburn was a thin man, a now impassive man who stood beneath the light, his long nose and cheekbones highlighted, and Sherwood thought: You'd make a good morgue attendant.

Sherwood said, "It's not that I'm interested in your work. It's my own that I'm trying to remember. Is there anything—"

"Please," Rayburn said, raising his hand again. "I can't discuss it."

"Why?"

"First, because I never knew what your work was— never cared to know—and second, Dr. Schlessenger has instructed me to discuss nothing with you."

"Why?"

Rayburn sighed. "I only work at the Institute, Doctor. I can't speak for the director's motives. As an employee I can only follow instructions."

Virginia said peevishly, "Isn't there any autonomy at the Institute?" for which she received only a cold stare.

"Look, Doctor," Sherwood said exasperatedly, "I'm only trying to piece together what I had here, trying to see if what I was doing had any bearing on my condition."

Rayburn replied stoically, "I'm afraid there is nothing I can say." He turned, opened the screen door. "Good night."

Virginia stepped to him, put a hand on his arm. "Doctor," she said, "a man's memory is at stake. Won't you help him regain it?"

Rayburn said to the door, "I would say, Mrs. Sherwood, that you could help him more than anyone."

"But you don't understand. I—"

"Let him go," Sherwood said sharply, taking Virginia's arm. "Thank you for nothing, Doctor." He walked her off the porch.

When they reached the car, Virginia demanded, "Now why did you do that? He was about ready to say something."

"And you were about ready to tell him you had amnesia."

"Well, what if I was? He might have talked."

"I don't think so. He sounds to me like Schlessenger's man and he'd run right to him with it."

"So?"

"So I run to Schlessenger with it instead and see what happens. Don't you see? One person has amnesia, but two persons have—what?"

"Maybe we should see him next."

"No let's see if he's primed some of the others."

They sat in the front seat of the car with the inside light on, examining the list of names Sherwood had compiled, remembered from the walk down the corridor of the Institute, the addresses copied from the Merrittville phone book Virginia held in her lap.

"Dr. Schlessenger lost no time in spreading the word," Virginia said, smoothing out the sheet on top of the book. "Do you really think there's any sense in trying to see any of the others?"

"He might not have reached them all. Besides, I'm interested in reaction. Here, let me have the list."

Virginia drew it out of his reach, smiling. "I'm in charge of routing, Dr. Sherwood, remember?" she said. "After all, I have a share in this, too."

"Well, then, get on with it," he said gruffly, dropping his hand to his coat pocket and fishing for a package of cigarettes. She was right; he'd have to get used to her and the fact that there were two Sherwoods now and that she was looking for missing years, too.

"Rayburn was the closest," she said. "Now there's Anthony Black. He lives on Wisteria Drive."

"All right, coordinator in charge of routing, where's that?"

"I'm looking." She opened the phone book to a map of Merrittville and vicinity. "It's west of town."

"That helps a lot."

"It's the last street off Main and wiggles around on the map. Is that better?"

"Much better," Sherwood said, starting the car.

The cottage on Wisteria Drive was dark and they debated for a while before they decided to go up the walk and try the bell. There was no answer when they did.

"Well?" Sherwood said when they were in the car again.

"Hampton Cox is next," she said. "Twenty-eight Main Street. Do you think you can find that?"

The Hampton Coxes lived in an apartment over a music store on Main Street and were not reticent at all about talking. In fact, no sooner had Sherwood pressed the buzzer in the hallway on the main floor when a door at the top opened and a rotund man in a T-shirt appeared at the stairs and called, "Hi, Doc, Ginny," and started down the stairs in stocking feet. "Kitty and I've been expecting you.

Tried to call you a little while ago, but you weren't home. Figured you must be on your way." He jabbed out a hand and Sherwood took it. A head shorter than Sherwood, Cox gave him a piercing look from bright blue eyes in a jovial face, saying, "It's good to see you."

He walked them upstairs and into the living room, the Sherwoods coming face to face with Kitty, Cox's wife, as thin as he was fat, wearing an expression of good humor and nodding in friendly fashion as Cox said, "Sit down and be comfortable."

"You were expecting us, you said?" Sherwood asked as they sat on the davenport Cox indicated.

"As soon as. I heard you were back," Cox said, still standing. "Beer?"

"No, thanks," Sherwood said, not wanting to get sidetracked.

Cox dropped into an armchair and said, "What's it all about, Walt. What are you doing back in Merrittville?"

"Trying to find something."

"Schlessenger says you're trying to find your memory."

"He told you?"

"He says you can't remember a damn thing. Is that true?"

"Yes."

"You don't remember us—Kitty and me?"

"No."

Kitty gave a little gasp. Cox whistled a low note and said, "I'll be damned. I thought maybe Schless was giving me the business. I never know how to take that man."

Sherwood said, "He did talk to you, though?"

Cox nodded. "He said I shouldn't tell you anything. Now that just doesn't make sense, if you ask me."

"Why?"

119

"You ought to be entitled to information. After all, you worked there for a long time. Whatever made you quit, anyway?"

"I don't know."

"Of course you wouldn't know, having forgotten everything." Cox went on ruefully, "I wish I had the guts to get out. Great White Father Schlessenger. He gives me a pain sometimes. Right where I sit down."

"Hamp!"

"Well, it's true, Kitty."

"Evidently you don't like him, Mr. Cox," Virginia said. Cox stared at her. "'Mr. Cox'? You never used to call me that, Ginny. What's happened to you?"

There was no way out. "It so happens," Sherwood said, "that she has lost her memory, too."

"Oh, now," Cox said, running a hand through his thinning hair, "that's going a little too far. You can't expect us to believe—"

Kitty said solemnly, "I think it's true. You don't remember me, do you, Ginny?"

"I'm afraid not," Virginia said.

"I had the feeling you didn't. No recognition in your eyes."

"Well, I'll be damned," Cox said. Then he said in an outraged voice, "It's a shame. A dirty shame. You know I thought you were both acting strange, but I thought it was just nerves."

"You were saying," Virginia pursued, "that you didn't like Dr. Schlessenger. Why?"

"Why? Oh, it's the way he does things. For example, late this afternoon he comes into the lab and says, 'Hampton, Walter's back and he's got amnesia.' Then he stops. Do you know why? To see what kind of an effect it has on me, whether I know anything about it, whether Doc's been to see me first or not. But I only stand there with my mouth open. So he goes on, 'He says he can't remember anything for the past eleven years. What do you think of that?' I learned long ago not to say anything. Let him take the lead. The last thing he said was, "If he should happen to come to see you, I'd appreciate it if you'd say nothing to him."

Sherwood asked, "What did you say to that?"

"Just grunted something, I don't remember what. Didn't promise a damn thing."

"Why do you suppose he doesn't want you to talk with Walter?" Virginia asked.

"I don't know. I've given up trying to figure Schless out. One minute he thinks everybody's stealing equipment and secrets and the next he's handing out bonuses. I think he's happiest when he's upset about something."

"Dr. Rayburn wouldn't talk with us," Sherwood said. "Why should you?"

Cox looked at him squarely. "Because you are a friend of mine and Schlessenger be damned. You and Ginny spent many a night with us, Walter."

Sherwood said warmly, "Well, I'm glad we've found two friends in Merrittville."

Cox leaned forward. "You and I, we knew each other. We weren't backbiters, and we weren't always at each other's throat. The rest of them out there are a bunch of sticks. Old Horse Face Rayburn doesn't talk to anybody but his trichina. Sometimes he gives me the willies. Kitty won't go near him. Black is almost as bad, just an Institute man with Schlessenger serving as his spinal column. Wilhelm and Heneberry are both new and younger, but they run when Schless says run and halt when he says halt.

You and I were the only real research men out there. The rest are just window dressing for the National Science Foundation, so much payroll padding."

"What about my work. Did you know anything about that?"

"Not much, Walt. We knew each other real well, but we didn't discuss each other's work very often. Yours wasn't in my life and vice versa."

"What's your line?"

"Radioactive poisons."

"And mine?"

"Brain stuff. Brain waves. Brain this and brain that. You were always putting somebody in the BEG room and running tests on him. Got tired of running Ollie through all the time, so you were always looking around for volunteers. Had me in there once. I think you were on to something. Old Schless was pretty excited about your work."

"You mentioned Ollie. Who's he?"

"He was a sort of whipping boy for the researchers but you used him most. I guess he liked you. Schless got rid of him after you quit. They had a row, I think. Ollie had only a B.S. I don't know what Schlessenger was paying him."

"Maybe this Ollie knew something."

"I don't know. Schless accused him of stealing equipment. He was just a kid."

"Local boy?"

Cox pursed his lips. "I don't think so." He turned to Kitty. "He wasn't a Merrittville boy, was he, Kit?"

"Detroit, I think."

"Anyway, I haven't seen him since Schless got back."

Sherwood said, "Just the same I'd like to know more about him. Do you think you could get his address for me?"

"Ought to." Cox grinned. "I could sneak a look at the files. There ought to be something on him." His eyes slid to Virginia and back to Sherwood again. "I can't get over it. You two act like zombies, do you know that? Relax. You're among friends. You used to say you could let your hair down at the Coxes. Only I could never get you over here often enough to do you much good."

Sherwood said, "If you were to guess, what would you say is responsible for our amnesia?"

Cox sighed. "I suppose I'd act the same way, Walt, if I were in your shoes. Wouldn't rest until I knew, so maybe telling you to relax is the wrong thing. As for what causes your amnesia—" He shook his head. "I wouldn't begin to know what to say."

Virginia said, "Do you think it could be connected with the laboratory?"

"Maybe."

"You said Walter was on to something, that Dr. Schlessenger was excited about his work."

"There doesn't seem to be any alternative, does there? Two people just don't go around becoming amnesiacs at the drop of a hat." Cox screwed up his face. "You could have hit on something that affects your memory, Walt. Maybe it didn't take effect, like radioactive poison, until you were way out in Los Angeles.

"But Ginny wasn't at the Institute," Kitty pointed out. "How could she get it?"

"That's right. I didn't think of that."

"I hope you won't mention Virginia's condition to Schlessenger," Sherwood said. "I want to tell him myself."

"Going to spring it on him, huh? Well, I won't spoil it."

"What about me?" Virginia said in a small voice.

"What about you?" Cox asked.

"What was I doing all this time? What did I do in Merrittville?"

Sherwood saw the glance that passed between Cox and his wife. Kitty said, "You worked out at the Institute some. Mostly for Dr. Wilhelm. You made routine counts for him."

"How about that beer now?" Cox asked suddenly.

"Coffee," Kitty said, darting him a look.

"Coffee," Cox said, beaten. "Always spoiling a good time. Kitty and her calorie charts. She can have it but won't take it, and I can't have it and want it."

Virginia said, "Maybe I can help you, Kitty," and rose.

When they were alone, Sherwood said quickly, "What was the look for, Hampton?"

Cox said with surprise, "Look?"

"The look you gave your wife when Virginia asked about what she did in Merrittville."

"I was afraid you noticed it."

"What did it mean?"

"You were a busy man, Walt."

"So?"

"You were always at the Institute. She wasn't happy about it. Used to spend a lot of time with Kitty." He was silent for a moment, then blurted out, "Ginny loves kids."

"I see." He felt Cox's mind inch away from his. "I never thought about children. Last week—eleven years ago—I was a single man."

"Well, if you ever start thinking about them, don't move over a music store. Too much interference from downstairs. We could have a house like Rayburn's, but we're salting our money away. Glad of it, too. Never can tell when you'll need it."

"Any reason for thinking that way?"

"Well, things haven't been going too well at the Institute. You knew about it."

"Something involving you?"

"Something involving us all, Walt." Cox seemed a little uncomfortable in the chair and shifted around. "In the first place, you have to understand that Schlessenger never had an original idea in his life. We all know that, of course. He started the Institute because he was unable to do any research himself—oh, he's qualified, has all the degrees and everything, though we often wonder just how he got them."

When Cox paused for a moment, Sherwood said, "Just a big faker, eh?"

"No, I wouldn't go so far as to say that, Walt. He's got spirit, he's got background, and he's impressive. Sometimes that's all you need in this business. He's a good front man and you've got to give him credit for that. Maybe that's all a director should be. Maybe we all expect too much. But anyway, he's found himself as the Chief, and he revels in it, although we all suffer more or less because he plays at it so hard. It was Georgia Schlessenger's money that got him the Institute, you know. Did you know that?"

"No."

"Well, it's true. She furnished most of the money and Schlessenger went after the rest of it from the National Science Foundation. He was happy and so was she when they got the go-ahead. He hired a couple of friends—Rayburn and Wilhelm—and he was in business. Then he hired Heneberry and Black, two other one-time acquaintances he wanted to impress. The result was, he got into trouble."

"Trouble?"

Cox nodded. "Nobody was producing anything. They were all doing what they damn well pleased and not a, thing more. No plan, no goal. A lot of their work was merely a repetition of what had already been done in their fields. Schlessenger thought they could get by that way and defended them, but it didn't work out. The National Science Foundation got on his back. Those boys wanted to see some results. They didn't care what it was just as long as it was something new and could satisfy the appropriation. They pointed out they weren't putting up money to prove what was in the textbooks. The upshot was that I was hired out of a University of Illinois lab where I was doing advanced work on radioactivity and then somebody told him about you and the next thing you knew you were on your way from Ryerson for Merrittville, Michigan.

"I've done a couple things along the lines of treatment for exposure to radiation, and I think you did a few things in your field, too, but not nearly enough to keep the Foundation happy. About a year ago we had a staff meeting, and we were all given orders to get to work on new ideas, something to make the Foundation think it was getting its money's worth. But as far as I know, Rayburn and Wilhelm are still puttering around with their old work, Heneberry and Black started in a half-dozen directions at once and have got exactly no place and I have months to go before I know if I've got anything."

Cox was silent for a moment. Then he said, "You were the closest to finishing a project and you quit before you completed it. You were always pretty touchy about your work. Schlessenger probably pressed you too hard."

The picture of Schlessenger was coming into focus. Sherwood said, "So now Schlessenger isn't sure he'll have anything when the Foundation asks for it, is that it?"

"The grapevine has it that he promised to produce a few weeks ago and that it was a sheer, bare-faced bluff. Now I understand he's asked the Foundation for more time. He's pushing us all, hoping for something, anything at all, so I suppose it's true."

"And if you don't come through with something you might be out of a job?"

Cox shrugged. "If Schless doesn't have anything to show, the Foundation will cut off the appropriation. It won't hurt Schlessenger, but it will put the rest of us on the dole."

"You don't think he'd continue without an appropriation?"

Smiling wryly, Cox said, "I'd hate like hell to count on it."

"How about this trip to California? How did that come about?"

"It was a convention. Santa Barbara this year. Last year it was Cleveland. All the neurophysiologists. You and Ginny went each year. In fact, Ginny lived the whole year for that. It was one time of the year when she'd have you all to herself—except that Schlessenger insisted on going along this year. Of course he always went to the conventions—his wife hated them, she says—but he'd always go with some big shot, never with one of the boys. I don't think your wife cared for the arrangement."

"Maybe that's why I quit."

"Why would you wait until you got to Los Angeles to do it?"

"I wonder if I'll ever know."

"We were all surprised as hell at the Institute when Schless came back without you. Nobody expected you to quit like that."

When they drew up in front of the house on Walnut Street and Sherwood turned off the lights and the motor, they both sat in the quiet car, Sherwood frowning at a lone street light a half block away, Virginia staring moodily and unseeing through the windshield, both reliving the past four hours with the Coxes.

He glanced at his watch. He couldn't see it very well, so he lit a cigarette and used the lighter to illuminate the dial. Twelve ten. Too late to see anybody else.

"What time is it?" Virginia asked.

"Ten minutes after twelve."

"Late."

"Wish it were earlier."

"Why?"

"I'd like to see Schlessenger right now."

"He's probably asleep."

"Not the way things are going at the Institute."

"What?"

He told her what Cox had said about Schlessenger, seeing her absorbed face turned toward him as he talked, the distant street light shining like a star in her eyes.

When he finished, she said, "I haven't changed my mind."

"About what?"

"Schlessenger."

"Your intuition still at work?"

"Yes. I don't think he's to be trusted. Especially after that business with the National Science Foundation. Why didn't he hire good men in the first place?"

"Perhaps he was trying to impress somebody. Maybe he didn't care, as long as he had the title of director."

They continued to sit in the car, lost in thought, until Virginia said, "Walter," and paused as if she were tasting the words before she said them, "are you going to see Schlessenger tomorrow?"

"Of course. And you're going along."

She lowered her eyes, let them slide to the dashboard. "What if your talk with Schlessenger doesn't do any good?"

"What do you mean?"

"What if it turns out he really doesn't know anything that will help you?"

"I don't see what you're driving at."

"I mean…supposing nothing works out. For us."

"It's got to work out, Virginia. There has to be an answer."

She reached out a hand and ran an exploratory finger around the chrome of the clock. "But if there isn't?"

He said firmly, "There will be."

"That's easy to say."

"You mustn't think of failure."

She turned to him. "I want to be ready for it."

"I don't even want to think about failing. I don't want to go along the rest of my life a—'a zombie,' as Cox said."

"I don't feel like a zombie."

"We're incomplete persons, you and I. Half people."

"Maybe we are," she said stubbornly, "but I don't feel like it."

He looked at her squarely. "Are you trying to say you're satisfied with the way things are?"

"I've just thought of being forced to go on living without ever learning about the hidden years, that's all."

"You mean you *want* it that way?"

She turned to meet his blinkless stare. "I mean I wonder if they're as important as we seem to think they are."

"Important? Why, they're the difference between being a neurophysiologist and a high school graduate, that's all. And for you—" He paused when he realized it would not mean so much to her.

"I know getting back your identity means a lot to you, Walter, but I want to know if you could go on like this if you had to, never knowing about those missing years."

He saw what the answer meant to her and he knew what he should say, but in a way the question angered him, so he said truthfully, "I don't know," and when he saw her look away after he said it, he wished he could cut his tongue out.

"I'm sorry," he said. "I meant—"

But this only made it worse.

CHAPTER THIRTEEN

WHEN VIRGINIA woke him to tell it was time for breakfast, how did he want his eggs, Sherwood thought *I suppose this is how it used to be, living in this house, getting up for breakfast, going out to the Institute, coming home each night. Except that Cox said I had little time for home. I can't imagine myself ignoring Virginia like that.*

He sat up in bed, looked out on a green backyard complete with arbor, hearing the sounds of birds in nearby trees. It was quiet, restful, and already warm for so early this July day, and for a moment he was reluctant to leave it, and he thought: *Maybe Virginia has a point, maybe we should leave well enough alone.* But he would not let himself get lost in this labyrinth of thought and swung his feet to the floor just as Virginia called from downstairs asking him if he was coming.

As it was, he stepped into the kitchen just as she was transferring his egg from frying pan to plate. He gave her a smile, pulled out her chair for her, and going around to his own, said, "I didn't expect anything like this."

She poured coffee, saying, "Maybe I'm setting a bad precedent."

"A good precedent, you mean."

"Maybe I should let you get your own breakfast."

"You wouldn't want to see me wither and die, would you?" He drank his orange juice. "Was all this here?"

"I've been to the store. What time do you think it is? People in Merrittville get up early."

He glanced at the kitchen clock. Nine twenty. "By Institution standards I suppose the day's well under way."

He had just started on his egg when the phone rang. For a moment they sat in startled silence looking at each other. Then Sherwood said, "So we have a phone."

"It's in the alcove beneath the stairs. I noticed it yesterday." She rose.

"I'll get it," he said.

It was Hampton Cox.

"I'm calling from downtown. I ran in for something and thought I'd call you."

"You've found out something?"

"In a way. Do you know that woman—Miss Lawson? She's Schlessenger's receptionist and secretary."

"Yes, I met her yesterday."

"She's always been friendly to me. I asked her this morning for Lansing's address."

"Lansing?" he said and then remembered this name as that of his lab assistant.

"Oliver Lansing. You know—Ollie."

"Oh. Did you get it?"

"No."

"No? Why?"

"She was as surprised as I. Every reference to him has been taken out of the files. It's as if he never worked at the Institute."

"I'll be damned."

"She was all for quizzing Schlessenger about it, but I told her she better not. Something's up, all right."

"Schlessenger got rid of it."

"What else is there to think, Walt? For some reason he doesn't want anybody to contact Ollie."

"He must know something then."

"A guy can't just disappear without leaving some trace. I know where he used to live here in town and I'm going to call Kitty. She can get on the telephone, call the post office, see if he left a forwarding address, nose around among people she knows. Something ought to turn up."

"You mentioned Detroit. You think he might have gone there?"

"You might try calling Detroit. Listen, I've got to get back. I'll let you know if anything else happens."

Virginia said, "Your eggs are cold," when he returned to the kitchen. "What was that all about?"

He told about Ollie and what Cox had discovered at the Institute. "It's the first real lead we've had."

"There must be a lot of Lansings in Detroit. You couldn't call them all. Besides, if this Ollie lived here he wouldn't have a phone listed in Detroit."

Sherwood agreed. "But Ollie is a young man. He may be a junior. If he is, then I'll get to him. It's worth the chance."

He finished his breakfast, had his hand on the phone to make the call to Detroit when the phone rang. It was Booey.

"It's between classes, Walter. I had to know about you. What have you found out?"

"Not much. Schlessenger at the Institute wasn't helpful."

"Still don't remember anything, eh?"

"Still a blank."

"Have you seen or heard anything of Virginia?"

"She's here. She was here when I got here."

"Well, then, what does she say?"

"I hate to tell you this, Doctor, but she's lost her memory, too."

"What?"

"I know it must sound fantastic to you."

"That's putting it mildly. What in the world is happening?"

"She thought I'd be able to help her, if you can imagine that."

"Walter, it's—things like this just don't happen."

"I know it."

"This is no mere amnesia."

"I think that too."

"It has something to do with your work. Something went wrong somewhere. Have you investigated that at all?"

"Schlessenger's pretty close-mouthed about what I was doing."

"I'd open his mouth if I were you. Use a crowbar if you have to. He's sitting on something."

"That's what we think. We're going out there this morning and tackle him again."

"Listen, Walter, I think I'd better come up."

"You're welcome to come if you want."

"You need help."

"I may need it before it's all over. I don't know just what you could do, but I'd appreciate any suggestions."

"It's a crime, that's what it is, this thing happening to two nice young people like you. You need to get at the bottom of it. Somebody's to blame and you need to know who it is."

"We're doing our best to find out."

"I'll be up. I'll put Scott in charge. Needs experience anyway. I'll be there as soon as I can."

Next Sherwood put in a call to Detroit, Michigan, to one Oliver Lansing. The operator said there was an Oliver

Lansing, Sr., listed on Craddock Road, she'd ring the number.

Mrs. Lansing answered. No, Oliver Lansing was not there, he was at work. No, Oliver Lansing, Jr., was not there, who was calling, please? When he told her who he was and where he was calling from she said she did not know where he was and broke the connection.

He tried calling back but the phone kept ringing.

Mrs. Lansing obviously did not wish to discuss her son's whereabouts.

Why?

"Well, this is a surprise," Schlessenger said when they were ushered into his presence. "Sherwood told me yesterday you deserted him, Mrs. Sherwood. I knew you wouldn't do a thing like that."

"I said I hadn't seen her," Sherwood corrected. "I didn't say she deserted me."

"No matter," Schlessenger said, getting up and moving another leather chair over to the desk. He saw them seated before he moved around to his own chair again, saying, "Mrs. Sherwood is here and that's what's important. When did you return?"

"I arrived late yesterday," Virginia said. "I was at home when Walter returned from seeing you."

"That's fine. Fine. Now I'm sure we'll get somewhere." He rubbed his hands together. "With you here, Walter will be coming out of it, I feel sure. Not that I'm trying to minimize anything, you understand. It's a grave case. Truly a grave case. I've been able to think of nothing else since yesterday. I presume he's told you everything?"

"Yes, he has."

"Did he tell you what I suggested?"

"Yes."

"Good. Now what have you decided?" Sherwood said, "Our plans depend on you."

"How's that?"

"We went to see some of the researchers last night. We dropped in on Rayburn first."

"Oh?" Schlessenger's eyelids flickered ever so slightly. "Now why did you do that?"

"Perhaps you'd better tell us why you told him not to tell us anything."

"It's a policy here that information should come from me. I merely wanted to remind him of that. I don't like to have my researchers interfered with. I might say I've kept plenty of people off your tail, Walter, if you only knew it. I'm sure your wife will attest to that."

"I'd hardly call what you did last night a friendly move," Sherwood said crisply.

"You were a mighty confused man yesterday, Walter. I didn't know what you were going to do when you left here. I can't see how you could blame me for not wanting any of my key men disturbed."

"Were you afraid I would discover something?"

"You imply there is something to discover, which there isn't. It was only a move to insure their preparation. I think they have a right to know what's going on. I don't like trouble, Walter." He turned to Virginia. "Surely you can see the sense of it, Mrs. Sherwood."

Virginia's face signified nothing.

"We also went to see Dr. Black," Sherwood said.

"Is that so? What did he have to say?"

"He wasn't home. But Dr. Cox was."

"A good man, Hampton. A little high strung, but a good clinician, a good lab man."

"We got along pretty well."

"You two always did, Walter. Hampton is a friendly chap. But why did you bother to see these people? I can tell you anything you want to know. Didn't you tell Walter that, Mrs. Sherwood?"

Virginia met his gaze coolly. "I didn't say so," she said, "but I'm sure you can." She smiled and Schlessenger seemed for the moment a little puzzled by the answer.

"Well," he said gruffly, "I'm glad of that. Now tell me, have you thought about what ought to be done?"

"Yes, Doctor. But we thought we'd leave that up to you. What would you suggest?"

And Sherwood thought: *That's the girl, hand it back to him.*

"Why, treatment, of course, just as I suggested. The best treatment." He brought his chair up and leaned toward them, folding his hands on the desktop. "It so happens I have a number of specialist friends…"

"If there is going to be treatment," Sherwood said emphatically, "it will have to be for both of us."

"Both of you?" He chuckled. "You want her along to hold your hand, I suppose. Is that it?"

"That's not what I mean."

"I was just joking, Walter." Schlessenger coughed politely. "Actually, I think it would be best. She can fill in the gaps for the psychiatrist if there is to be narcosynthesis."

"That's still not what I mean," Sherwood said evenly.

"Well, what *do* you mean?" Schlessenger said sharply.

When Sherwood said nothing, he went on, "Don't sit there with that silly smile on your face. You think you know something. What is it?"

"Virginia doesn't remember any more than I do."

Schlessenger's face went hard and his eyes, narrowed so quickly in suspicion, jumped from one to the other. Very ugly, he said, "Just what are you two trying to pull off here?"

"We're not trying to pull anything off," Sherwood said calmly. "It happens to be true."

"Don't make me laugh." He got up suddenly, walked grimly around the desk as if to go to the bar, then turned silently on the thick rug and leaned on the desk. "Is this true, Mrs. Sherwood?"

"Yes, it's true."

The arms came up and he turned away from them, leaning his rump against the desk, staring across the room. Presently he said, "I don't like this."

"*You* don't like it?" Sherwood said cuttingly, "How do you suppose we feel about it?"

"How the hell should I know," Schlessenger said, whirling around. "I've never had amnesia."

"Haven't you?" Sherwood said, rising. "You seemed to have it yesterday when you couldn't remember anything about my work."

"Quit talking as if I were responsible for your condition, Walter. As for your work, you admitted to me yesterday you felt like a stranger here. Why then should I tell a stranger anything? Besides, I did tell you a few things but you lacked the memory background to assimilate them."

"Just so much gobbledygook."

"It was *not* gobbledygook." He turned away, walking to the bar, hands in his coat pockets, his body taut with in-held wrath. When he turned around, he said quietly, "One person with amnesia I can understand, even though there is no bona fide way to prove whether he is telling the truth, but *two* persons—"

"You think we're faking!"

"I didn't say it," Schlessenger said fiercely. "You did."

"You thought it, Doctor," Virginia said pointedly.

"I'm just stating a fact well known in psychiatry. Amnesia is as unprovable as backache, that's all. To go on, I can believe one person can have amnesia and I can believe one person can pretend to have amnesia. But when someone tries to tell me a man and wife can have amnesia together, well," he laughed a dry laugh, "it just can't be, that's all."

"It is a fact, Doctor," Virginia said doggedly. "Not only do we both have amnesia, but we happened to contact it at exactly the same time in the same place."

Schlessenger lit a cigarette, blew out smoke to obliterate the flame and studied the lighter. He said tightly, "Walter, if it weren't for the fact that to you I'm a stranger—or so you say—I'd throw you out of here."

Gripping the arms of his chair, Sherwood said combatively, "I would like to see you try that, Doctor." Schlessenger ignored him by going on. "As it is, I happen to have done things for you that render you forever in my debt, whether you know it or not. I gave you your chance to work in research that interests you and I didn't interfere. On the contrary, I encouraged you, helped you, boasted about you, told some of my friends high in government and other research centers about you."

"What does all that mean?"

"It means this, Walter: you have no right to come in here making rash accusations like that. Particularly since I've offered to help you all I can."

"When does this so-called help commence?"

"Will you be quiet long enough for me to tell you?" He put down the lighter. His eyes were brighter than they had been. "I wasn't quite frank with you yesterday, Walter. The reason is that since only you were affected there might be no tie-up and there was no sense revealing Institute business because of such an improbable connection. But in view of your condition—er—conditions…"

He leaned back in the chair, scowled at the ceiling. "I think you have learned enough about yourself to know you were a brilliant man. You were what I wanted in a research man. The hell of it is you were even more than that. You were able to work not only on projects which we discussed and to which you were assigned but also on some things of your own. Our main difficulty, yours and mine, was agreeing on what was Institute business and what comprised your own private pursuits. You so often overstepped the limits of experimentation set by the Institute that I suppose I paid more attention to you than to the others."

Schlessenger moved forward, deftly deposited ashes in the tray on the desk, wiping away a solitary speck of ash from the desktop with a fingertip. "As a result, I know you were working on something you didn't want any of us to know about. When I asked you about it you denied it, but I wasn't fooled. Not for a minute. You knew how I felt about it so you were careful to conceal everything. But one day I came in when you were in the middle of something you wouldn't let me see. I told you then it was either let me know what it was or abandon it for Institute work. I told you if you felt so strongly about it to take it home and work on it there, whatever it was. You said you couldn't do that, if that was the way I felt about it, you'd abandon it."

He faced Sherwood squarely. "I don't think you really abandoned it at all, Walter. The reason you spent so much time out here was to be able to work on it when no one was here, which was often late at night. I think the reason you quit was you had finished it, whatever it was, or had nearly finished it, and didn't wish to be associated with the Institute when whatever it was would be revealed."

Schlessenger squashed the cigarette and sighed. "We'll never know what it was, Walter, because it backfired, and the way you and Mrs. Sherwood are is evidence of it. The pity of it is that there is no one to help you because you never confided in anyone.

"But that's all just guess, isn't it, Doctor?" Virginia said hopefully.

"You see the wet grass and the streets when you come out of a movie," Schlessenger said, "so you know it's been raining. A simple deduction."

"Why didn't you tell me about this yesterday?" Sherwood demanded.

Schlessenger said patiently, "Yesterday there was no basis for thinking your amnesia was caused by anything more than overwork or concern. Today, with Mrs. Sherwood suffering from exactly the same thing, I can't think anything else. It is the only explanation."

Virginia said, "Surely Walter discussed it with someone."

"He might have discussed it with you," Schlessenger said. "Perhaps he left notes."

"Not Walter. He used no notes. He had an extraordinary power of recall. And there's nothing in the laboratory, if that's what you're going to suggest next. It has had a thorough cleaning."

"Search, you mean," Sherwood said bitingly. "You'd have given your right arm to know what it was."

Schlessenger smiled thinly. "The Institute can always use a new development as proof of its efficacy."

"What about this person called Ollie?" Virginia asked. "He used to help Walter."

Schlessenger snorted. "Oliver Lansing was a kid fresh from college who couldn't decide whether he liked girls or science more. He got into everybody's hair around here. Unfortunately he had itchy fingers. He wasn't making enough money so he picked up laboratory equipment and sold it to a fence in Detroit."

"So you fired him."

Schlessenger nodded. "I fired him."

"Tell me, Doctor, is it the usual practice when you fire someone to completely remove his records from your files?"

"In such cases, yes. It would not do to have a blot on, the Institute. Appropriations have been withdrawn for less. But how would you know about that?"

"I've been spying."

"I must tighten security out here," Schlessenger said, smiling. "If you had come to me, I could have told you that. Why is it you insist on getting your information from others?" In the next moment he was on his feet and coming around the desk. "Look, both of you. I want you to feel free to come out here any time. I'll answer all your questions as well as I can, and I'll try not to confuse you if they get technical. I don't want you to feel that I am against you."

He placed a hand on Sherwood's shoulder. "I want you both to take treatment. In case it turns out doctors can do nothing for you, I want you to think about going back to school. It's not too late. I will personally underwrite both the treatment and the school. Do you realize that in a few years you could be back where you were with the same knowledge you had before?"

They left Schlessenger and walked glumly through the hissing door to the driveway, crunching down the loose gravel, Sherwood with his fists in his pockets and she with an arm in his.

In the car he sat with the key in his hand, looking at the low-slung Institute building and saying, "Always an answer, hasn't he?"

Virginia sighed tiredly. "I feel he has a lifetime of practice behind him."

"Meaning?"

"Meaning my intuition tells me there's more to Schlessenger than meets the eye. That plus a little of the kind of deduction he mentioned."

He turned to her. "I know he's lying but I couldn't tell you why. If you have anything that's logical, let's hear it."

"All right. Suppose you are the director of an Institute like this."

"OK. I'm supposing."

"You arrange money from the National Science Foundation and you hire a man just like you."

"Go on."

"Suddenly one day this researcher punches a hole in his memory."

"An eleven year hole?"

"An eleven year hole."

"I could think it was amnesia."

She nodded. "It might even be reasonable, in view of how hard this researcher worked."

"All right."

"Now it so happens that the researcher's wife has an eleven year hole punched in her memory too and together the man and his wife go to the director and tell him. You're the director. What do you do?"

"I wonder about it." Sherwood scowled. "I begin looking up everything he knows about brain waves and that secret project he was working on. I see the possible connection."

"Do you say, 'Look, Mr. Researcher and wife, I'm sorry about all this, really I am. I want to send you to some psychiatrist friend of mine. Maybe he can help you. And if he can't, I'll pay—pay, mind you—for your re-education?'"

"No," Sherwood said. "I certainly do not."

"What do you do?"

"I see this as a new discovery, I question them thoroughly, I talk with everyone they knew, I search the laboratory, I search the house, I go over every inch of ground trying to find out what it is this researcher has discovered."

"And you don't send them out in the world with a pat on the back?"

"No. I tell them to keep in touch. I tell them that at the first glimmer of recollection to call me up day or night." Sherwood nodded. "I see what you mean."

"And furthermore," Virginia went on, "nobody's searched the house, nobody's talked to our friends."

"In short," Sherwood concluded, "Schlessenger's not interested. Why?"

"A good question, Doctor." She squirmed down into the seat. "Now, if you please, take me home. I have a lot of cleaning to do."

"Cleaning!"

"Yes, cleaning. If you ever want to think something out, just start housecleaning. It works every time. Ought to try it some time."

CHAPTER FOURTEEN

SHERWOOD found Georgia Schlessenger in the flower garden in the rear of the substantial Schlessenger residence, a long, elaborate structure that made much use of angels, pitched roof, floor-to-roof glass panes, planting boxes, and a two-car garage. A convertible Cadillac was on the driveway. The other car was undoubtedly at the Institute.

He had tried ringing the bell, and though he heard the chime, no one came to the door, so he started around the house, taking the flower-lined flagstone walk to the rear. He did not see her at first because she was crouched at the far end of the yard, working the soil with a trowel, a small figure in black slacks and blouse, a Mexican hat hiding her face.

He started toward her across the neatly trimmed lawn and saw her turn, stop what she was doing to watch him until he was within easy speaking distance. Only then did she forsake her work and rise, her face remarkably white for a woman who worked in a yard, a wondering face filled with freckles and two large eyes of a strange brown. He saw her hair now, saw that it had a reddish tinge beneath the hat, saw her freckled arms, her work-gloved hands. She looked upset.

"Dr. Sherwood," she said simply.

"I rang," he said, "but no one came. I saw the car and knew—"

"Oh, I never answer the chime." She brushed a lock of hair back up under the crown of the hat with an ungloved hand.

"I'd like to talk to you, Mrs. Schlessenger."

"Really?" She made no move to leave the garden. "Why?"

"It's about yesterday."

She looked down at the glove she was working off her other hand. "I would like to forget about yesterday."

"You wanted to tell me something."

"Did I?" The eyes came up, challenging. "Whatever gave you that idea?"

"You seemed upset there at the car, and when I tried to find out what was wrong you ran away."

"I suppose it did seem odd." She turned a little to drop the white gloves beside the trowel at the lawn's edge. "But you must forget it, Doctor. There was nothing to it really."

"Why did you run away?"

She glanced up at the sky where the sun was advancing to a mid-point in the heavens. "It's too hot out here to talk. Shall we go inside?"

She led the way across the lawn to the rear of the house. "Can I get you a drink?" she asked when they were in the kitchen. And when he said she could, she busied herself at the task, stopping at a cabinet and withdrawing a bottle. "Bourbon all right? There's scotch in the living room bar if you'd rather."

"No. Bourbon will be fine."

"How's your wife?"

"She's fine."

"I always liked Mrs. Sherwood." She broke a tray of ice cubes, and with silver tongs carefully withdrew two cubes for his glass before filling her own. "Of course I like you both. Andrew thinks a lot of you, too." Now she measured the bourbon, tossed it in on the ice. "Ginger ale?"

He nodded. She poured and stirred and then handed him his glass. "I'm sorry to hear of what's happened," she said. "Truly sorry."

They drank a little, their eyes not leaving each other, Sherwood's cool and curious, hers a little wide and disturbed.

"What did you want to tell me yesterday?"

"We're back to that?"

He nodded. "What was it?"

"You misunderstood. It was nothing." She held her drink in both hands and seemed to be forcing herself to look at him. "What are you and your wife going to do now?"

"Why don't you want to tell me?"

"Please," she said pleadingly into her drink. "I asked you what you and your wife are going to do now."

"There *was* something then."

"Will you stop? I told you you misunderstood. It was nothing. Nothing."

He said calmly, "I don't believe it."

She muttered, "Don't believe it, then."

"Dr. Schlessenger has told you about me?"

"Of course, he has." She would not look up.

"He told you I don't remember anything for the past eleven years."

"Yes."

"Did he tell you about Virginia, too?" She looked up with startled eyes.

He said, "Did he tell you she can't remember either?"

"Yes."

"When did he tell you that?"

"I don't know!" She stood up, glaring at him. "Walter, I want you to stop this. I'm not in the witness chair. I don't have to answer all this! You don't have the right—"

He smiled. "Why are you so upset?"

"Why are you asking me all these questions?"

"What do you know about what's happened to Virginia and me? What is it that Dr. Schlessenger won't tell me? What was it you were going to tell me yesterday?"

He watched her face, a pale, gaunt face with the freckles much more in evidence now, and he saw her pulse in her neck, beating fast, and he watched her sink resignedly into a chair opposite him, staring at the drink she put down on the table.

"Andrew is my husband," she said harshly, coldly. "I don't like what you're implying."

"What is it I'm implying?"

"Stop it. I told you I had nothing to say."

"Have you ever had amnesia, Mrs. Schlessenger?"

"No."

"Then you don't know what it feels like to be unable to remember, do you? Strange faces that look into your own, seeking something within you that you can't even find yourself."

"Please."

"Do you know what it's like? It's as if someone had put you into a time machine and moved you eleven years forward, as if you missed living completely those eleven years because you have no recollection of them."

"Walter I—"

"And then this girl beside you, the one that came back to you, you can see her and you're told she's your wife and you think my God what she must have meant to me but I don't even know it, don't even know what I must have meant to her. And you stand there, both of you unable to share the happiness you must have had. Do you know what it feels like to be like that?"

She turned grave eyes to him. "No—please..."

"And then," he said ruefully, "the crowning blow. The man who could help you says he's sorry but it's not his responsibility, that there's nothing he can do."

"But there *isn't* anything he can do?"

"Isn't there?" he asked fiercely. "No!"

"Well, *why* isn't there?"

"Because—!" And suddenly her face broke and she dropped her head to her hands and then sent her head and hands to the table, striking the glass and sending it crashing to the floor. Unmindful of this, she emitted a series of small cries from her throat, a soft sobbing that convulsed her.

Sherwood had not expected this. He stood and stared at her lowered head and shaking shoulders, uncertain now. He had gone too far, perhaps.

"Mrs. Schlessenger," he said gently.

"Oh, leave me alone," she moaned.

He waited patiently until the shoulders stopped shaking and she lifted her tear-stained face from the table, fumbling for and finding a Kleenex in her pocket and dabbing at her eyes with it.

"You'd better go," she said without emotion. She blew her nose gently. "I can't help you."

Virginia was not at home when he got there, which gave Sherwood a start and made him realize how much he had already come to depend on her. He had expected her to be surrounded by soap suds, mops and polish, and to be deep in thought, and he wondered if she had forsaken the cleaning to pursue some line of investigation that had occurred to her in the middle of her job.

But he had no time to wonder about it. The phone jangled him out of it.

"This is Kitty," the breathless voice said. "I've been trying to run down Ollie. Hamp told me to call if I found out anything."

"Any luck?"

"Yes. Ollie was fired by Dr. Schlessenger all right, and he did move out of his rooming house and go home, but he didn't stay long in Detroit."

"Where is he now?"

"Right here in Merrittville."

"Back here?"

"Yes. You see—" Pause. "Well, there's a girl."

"Oh."

"Her name's Gloria Conners. She lives over on Dempster Street."

"Where's that? Do you know if he's there now?"

"No, he's not there now. I just got through talking to him—"

"Where did he go? I've got to see him."

"You'll see him soon. He's coming over to your place." The front door chime sounded.

He said, "There's the door. I think he's here now. Goodbye. And thanks, Kitty."

But it wasn't Ollie.

It was Virginia, her arms full of groceries. She gave him an odd look. "What's the matter with you, Walter? You look feverish. Did something happen?"

He held the door open for her. "Ollie's coming."

"Oliver Lansing? Good." She walked past him, saying, "Surprised to find me gone?" and headed toward the kitchen.

"I thought you'd deserted me," he said, following her.

"I came home with the best of intentions, but I spied all those letters on the table. Mostly bills, so I paid them. Gas bill, light bill—did you know they hadn't been paid for two months?—water bill, safety deposit box rental—we each have a key, I learned—grocery bill, payment to the savings and loan—we own this house, did you know that? Or should I say we have an equity in it. The whole trip took almost all the money I had. Oh, and I picked up a few things for lunch, too. How did things go with Mrs. Schlessenger?"

"She went to pieces. The real news is Ollie. Kitty found out he's been in Merrittville most of the time since he was fired. He has a girl friend here."

She stopped in her task of putting the groceries away long enough to say, "I hope you're not disappointed, Walter."

"Disappointed?"

"I mean I hope you're not expecting Ollie to know too much."

"I'll be grateful if he remembers anything at all."

He watched her as she moved about the kitchen looking cool and pretty and as if she belonged there, which she did, and he thought: She looks happy I don't think she cares too much one way or the other in fact I know she doesn't.

"What's Mrs. Schlessenger like?"

"Oh, she's got freckles, brown eyes—"

Virginia gave him a withering look. "You know that's not what I mean."

"Oh, I found her working in the garden. We went in the house and had a drink. When I started to question her about her husband she got hysterical."

"So she knows, too. Do you like corned beef loaf?"

Before he could answer there were footsteps on the porch, the sound of the chime.

"Ollie," Sherwood said, turning to go.

A thin, solemn young man with a pockmarked, owlish face stood on the porch, his large gray eyes friendly and guileless. He was nearly as tall as Sherwood, but he was angular, his open-collared gray shirt hung loosely on his frame and his wrinkled brown slacks had slipped a little from his waist toward his hips.

"Hello, Doctor," he said gruffly in a low voice that was at once in variance with his years.

"Hello," Sherwood said. "Come on in. We've been waiting for you." He held the door open.

The gray eyes swept past Sherwood. "Afternoon, Mrs. Sherwood," he said with a nod.

"Hello, Ollie," Virginia said. Ollie darted a questioning look at Sherwood, a ghost of a smile crossed his face, and then he walked through the door.

"You've talked to Kitty," Sherwood said when they were inside and he was drawing a chair from the wall for him.

"Yes," Ollie said. "Kitty told me all about it." He sat down awkwardly.

Like a schoolboy, Sherwood thought. He sits there like a schoolboy uncomfortable at being invited to the schoolmaster's house. Seeing him there like that, he began to doubt he would be much help.

"Have you had lunch?" Virginia asked.

"Why, no ma'am, I haven't."

Sherwood could not wait. "I understand you used to help me in the lab, Ollie. Is that right?"

"Yes," Ollie said.

"We thought you might be able to help, shed some light on things."

"On how you lost your memories, you mean?"

"Yes," Sherwood said, groaning inwardly. There would be no revelation here, he thought.

But he was wrong.

"Well," Ollie said, looking from one to the other, "I guess you might as well know you're victims of the Sherwood Effect."

CHAPTER FIFTEEN

IT WAS A MOMENT that changed things, much as the moment of waking in the Coronado had altered his life, obfuscating it, and all the little moments since then that had illuminated sections of it and brought them into sharp relief, but never quite completing the picture, each revelation dependent upon the next, like moves in a treasure hunt, a never-ending chain, a thread that had to end somewhere and he thought does it really end somewhere maybe it goes on and on compounding itself into an algebraic complexity of things, a progression into infinity.

"The Sherwood Effect," Virginia said slowly, as if tasting the words.

"Yes, ma'am," Ollie said matter-of-factly. "Maybe you've heard of some others—the Ramsauer Effect, the Compton Effect, Raman Effect. Dr. Sherwood called his the Sherwood Effect."

"Just what is this Sherwood Effect?" Sherwood said.

Ollie smiled wanly and looked down at his hands. "It's nothing I can tell you right off the bat like that. I—I don't know how to start telling it."

"Why not try starting at the beginning?" Virginia said sensibly.

"Well, I don't know." Ollie looked at her, considered the suggestion and then swallowed. "I'll try." He became conscious of his hands and fiddled with them as he talked. "I started work at the Institute about a year ago. A little longer than that, maybe, but that's close enough." He looked up from his fingers.

"I was supposed to help everybody, Dr. Schlessenger said. You see, I wanted to work for a year or so to get money to go on and get my master's degree. I had a B.S. One of my teachers at the University—that's the University of Detroit—knew Dr. Schlessenger. He's pretty well known, you know. Anyway, that's how I got the job. You've got to do things like that if you're going to get what you want."

He paused.

"We understand," Sherwood said encouragingly.

"The way it was supposed to work out was they were to use me any time they wanted, any way they wanted. I tried to be impartial about it, just as Dr. Schlessenger told me to be, but I couldn't get along with Rayburn and Black. Wilhelm and Heneberry—they were only a few years older than I and I think it kind of embarrassed them to ask me to help them. So that left only Cox and you. But I was more interested in your work. It was closer to what I had liked—neurophysiology. And you'd answer my questions. Those other researchers, they'd just grunt when you asked them something. They pretended they were big wheels. But you weren't like that."

"I'm glad to hear that," Sherwood said. "I'm sure you were a great help to me."

"I'd like to think I was," Ollie said shyly.

"What kind of work was I doing?"

"Your work, as I said, was more interesting than the rest. As far as I could see, the rest of them were doing regular things, checking up on this and that—stuff I'd just gone through in school. I couldn't figure that out, Dr. Schlessenger letting them get away with that. You and Cox were the only real men out there. And you, Dr. Sherwood, you had ideas. Real ideas. Exciting ones. You used to talk about them all the time, though sometimes I thought you were talking more to yourself than to me. You know what I mean—daydreaming."

"What kind of ideas were they, Ollie?" Virginia asked. "Well," Ollie said, frowning at Sherwood, "that's what makes it so hard to explain. But take that stuff at first about Fritsch and Hitzig and their experiments in eighteen seventy. Or maybe that's going too far back."

"Fritsch and Hitzig?"

"They were scientists. Nineteenth century scientists. They worked with a dog." He gave Sherwood a calculating look and plunged into it in a rush of words. "What they did was apply an electrical current to the exposed frontal cortex of a dog and the anesthetized dog moved the leg on the opposite side of his body."

"I see," Sherwood said, impressed at the sudden change in the choice of words. "Go on."

"Well, you were interested in brain waves. You had an idea you could stimulate a brain to receive a mental image like a TV set. But you never got that far. You ran into the Sherwood Effect."

"The Sherwood Effect again."

"Yes. I'm afraid I'm not explaining this very well."

"You're doing fine."

Ollie wet his lips. "In epileptic seizure one of the brain's electrical discharges gets out of rhythm with the rest of the brain. You told me that. You said it occurs in the ganglion cells and moves out, spreading higher voltages over neighboring areas and causes hallucinations or body movements."

Ollie stopped again and when no one said anything he went on. "You were trying to find out what causes some of the more common mental aberrations. You had an idea you could correct disorders with the proper stimulus, supplying the correct cortical rhythms to offset the breakdown symptoms."

Sherwood nodded. "I had a drive in that direction. It started with my father and firmed with my experience in the army."

"You told me about it. You were crazy to find it and you were awfully close to it." He blushed. "I didn't mean that the way it sounded."

"Forget it. How did I go about it?"

"We studied—or rather you studied and I helped— Rahm stimulators and their waves. You know, those sawed-off ones. They have a rising phase. Lasts only a fraction of a millisecond." Ollie moved forward in the chair, his hands forgotten, his speech no longer slow and halting. "We studied thyratron stimulators, too. Doctor. They can stimulate certain actions, you know—like eye movements. You do it by touching a certain point in the brain—the anterior half of the precentralgyrus, to be exact. It was exciting. You thought you were on the threshold of something."

"It must have been exciting," Virginia said. "You're even making me feel it."

"Well, Doctor, you used to say, 'Look what we can do with a brain in front of us, an open brain into which we can poke a needle.' And then you'd look at me and say, 'Ollie, why can't we do the same thing from a distance?' See? You were really talking to yourself, but I was there. 'We could give people hallucinations. Maybe if we reversed the whole thing we could take hallucinations away.' You really believed there could be some neuronal activation of the temporal cortex from an external source."

Ollie coughed a little self-consciously and went on. "The secret, you said, was in the thalamus. We're continually bombarded by stimuli, you know, but few of them ever get by the thalamus. You used to tell me how it was like a jukebox that would play a record only if the coin was a real one. You figured if you could influence the thalamus to accept a fake coin-stimulus-you'd have the problem solved."

"Tell me something, Ollie," Sherwood said, "did Dr. Schlessenger know about this?"

"About your work?"

"About this project."

"Sure. Of course he knew. Why?"

"Nothing. Go on."

"Well, your theory was to attack the thalamus through sympathetic vibrations, cortical rhythms. Radio waves and other types of electromagnetic radiation just go right through our brains, you know, right through the thalamus, just as radio waves fail to activate a radio not tuned to receive them. So your idea was to duplicate cortical rhythms.

"In the lab you had an electronic stroboscope. A toposcope, it's called. You could make people feel they were having an epileptic seizure by flashing it in synchronization with the person's own brain waves. Not that that hadn't ever been done before. You just pointed out that it was a step in the direction of getting out of the brain and influencing it from a distance."

"I follow you," Sherwood said.

"Your next step was electromagnetic. You used a beat crystal oscillator that would deliver in the neighborhood of a million megacycles, using two quartz crystals of different frequencies so that their difference was a million megacycles. You had me running all over Detroit trying to get the right stuff for you."

"Now you've lost me," Sherwood said. "But no matter, just keep going."

"I'm not so sure about the rest of it. You said something about how you modulated this and suppressed all other frequencies with filters, and I think you mixed all this with still another crystal that provided a fifteen-cycle differential. That's a typical rhythm of the brain. You thought it would influence the thalamus, vibrating as it was with a beat of fifteen."

"You mean it didn't?"

"You put it all together, inserted it into a small leather case like they use for electrical test instruments, plugged it in like a shaver and tried to propagate your thoughts. I was right there in the lab when you first tried it."

"Did it work?"

"No."

"What *did* happen?"

"It didn't produce any thoughts or hallucinations. It just obliterated your memory. Same thing that a shock treatment does. Erases recall. Completely. Just like erasing a recorded piece of tape."

"So that's how it happened!"

"Yeah," Ollie said, sighing. "That's how it happened. You forgot everything you'd done for a whole week that first time, you had it on so long fiddling with it. It was just as though you'd never lived that week. Of course I had to try it. So you see?" He smiled and his thin face glowed. "I know just how you feel right now."

"At last we know," Virginia said softly.

"Yes, ma'am."

"I built a trap," Sherwood said, "and we fell in it." He withdrew a cigarette from a crumpled package in his pocket, lighted it absently, thinking why hadn't Schlessenger come right out and told them about it?

"There were some side effects," Ollie was saying. "You found using the memory suppressor made it easier for you to solve problems. I guess it gave your mind a rest; at least that's what you used to say. At night you'd set it to erase a week or so and the next morning your mind would be able, to cope with the problem you were trying to solve a lot better. Rested the mind, sharpened the memory. You said you found yourself remembering things you'd forgotten years ago, little things a person would never remember ordinarily—names and dates and numbers. You were pretty excited about this phase of it, the way it stirred up things in your head."

"I do remember things," Sherwood said. "I found out about that in California."

"You used to make it a game. You'd pick a certain date and try to remember everything you did on that day. I'd have to ask you all sorts of questions. You figured out a lot of uses for the suppressor-stimulator. You planned to use it to raise I.Q.s and you saw an immediate use for it in the psychiatric field."

"In what way, Ollie?" Virginia asked.

"Dr. Sherwood thought it would supplant hypnotism and narcosynthesis—and work a lot better—in helping patients recall psychological traumas. There were other allied applications, too."

"The short, exciting career of Dr. Walter Evan Sherwood," Sherwood said bitterly. "I committed mental suicide and took Virginia along with me."

It was suddenly quiet in the living room, lunch forgotten, three minds occupied with all that had occurred.

Then Virginia said, "What about Dr. Schlessenger? Where does he fit in all this?"

"He was trouble, ma'am. Just plain trouble. With a capital T. He was always there just when we didn't want him, in the way, asking questions, prying, making suggestions. It finally got so we didn't pay any attention to him. That made him angry. He didn't bother us too much at first, but when he found out what Dr. Sherwood was doing he got all excited. I mean about the TV idea, trying to broadcast into other people's minds. He was awfully disappointed when it didn't work, but when Dr. Sherwood told him about the suppressor-stimulator aspect of it, he bounced back again. Wouldn't let Dr. Sherwood rest, kept nagging him all the time to perfect it."

Sherwood said, "So he knew all about it, how it worked and everything."

"Oh, no. You told him you hadn't worked it out the way you wanted it yet. You told him it would be dangerous to try to do anything with it the way it was. You wanted to set up a controlled project, you wanted to make sure it affected all minds the same way, but Dr. Schlessenger was all for announcing it right away. He got plenty mad when you wouldn't go along. Then he started hounding you to put everything down on paper, but you knew why he wanted you to do that, so you told him you wouldn't. As it was he kept poking around in the lab when you weren't there, trying to find your notes, but you never left anything lying around. You'd even take the outfit home with you at night."

Sherwood rose and crossed to an ashtray on a table by the stairs and jammed his cigarette down hard in it. "Did I ever put anything in that safe in the lab?"

"Sure, but you wouldn't put this in it. You knew Dr. Schlessenger would find it there and you didn't want him monkeying with it until you were ready."

"I think I see now what happened," Sherwood said. "When convention time came, I had to put the device somewhere, so it was logical I would put it in the safe. I probably figured that since Schlessenger was coming along to the west coast it would be safe there. Only he managed to get it out of the safe and take it along and somehow use it out there to erase eleven years of our lives."

"We know what the disease is and how we came to get it," Virginia said dismally, "but we don't know how to get over it."

"Get over it?" Ollie said. "Why, the memory circuits needn't be suppressed forever."

Sherwood looked at him sharply. "You mean our memories will be coming back?"

"Not without the suppressor-stimulator they won't. It works both ways, you see. I guess I didn't make that part of it very clear. You can lock or unlock your memory, suppress or activate the circuits at will." He grinned. "It was weeks before you worked out the details so you could recover the memory of that week you lost when you first tried it. That's when you discovered it not only brought back what you had suppressed but a lot of other memories as well, memories you had long forgotten."

"Then all we need is this little machine, is that it?"

"Yes, ma'am."

"And Schlessenger's got it," Sherwood said quietly.

"Are you sure, Walter?"

"Of course. Where's your intuition? He has to have it."

"You think it's in the safe?"

"Probably not." Sherwood sat on the steps to the upstairs, lips between forefinger and thumb, scowling at the cracks in the old oak floor. "Let's figure it out. Dr. Schlessenger wants the suppressor-stimulator because…"

"He'll raise his own I.Q.," Virginia said.

Sherwood nodded. "And he'll stimulate his memory. He'll get total recall."

Ollie said, "One of the possible applications which may have interested Dr. Schlessenger was suggested by himself. He once said he could see an entire army rendered impotent when exposed to memory suppression. But he didn't know then how weak the emanations are. To do what he suggested, you said he'd have to have a suppressor-stimulator the size of a large building. You also said it was ridiculous to think in terms of a weapon, that you hadn't worked on it for that."

"How near to the outfit do you have to be to get the benefit—or the injurious effects, as the case may be—of the suppressor-stimulator?"

"A few feet at the most. After that its effect falls off rapidly. At six feet there would be no appreciable effect."

"All right," Sherwood got up, walked slowly across the room, turned around and continued walking to and fro, saying, "The way I see it, he brings the suppressor along to California. He doesn't know just when he'll use it, but he knows he will somewhere, somehow. Once in the motel, with the convention in Santa Barbara the next day, he knows he'd better use it. He might not get a better opportunity. The set-up is a natural."

Virginia said gravely, "Are you suggesting that he sneaked in and erased our memories during the night?"

Sherwood smiled. "Not at all. I think I know how he did it."

"How?"

Sherwood turned to Ollie. "How long would it take to erase eleven years from a person's life?"

"Five or six hours. We found you erase about a week with each half minute—same for coming out of it, too."

Virginia shook her head. "I can't see Dr. Schlessenger sneaking in, leaving the machine and coming back for it in six hours."

"Of course not," Sherwood said. "That would be too risky for Schlessenger. He'd never take a chance like that. But I know how he could do it without ever leaving his room."

"Our rooms joined," Virginia said. "I see how."

"Of course. He probably visited us, saw where the head of our bed was, right next to the wall separating our rooms, knew at once this was the opportunity he was looking for. He sets up the machine in his place right next to the wall and the outfit works through the wall on us, Schlessenger staying as far away from it as possible.

And I didn't quit my job out there," Sherwood said. "That was a lie."

"I never thought you quit," Ollie said. "I thought, when Dr. Schlessenger came back with the story that you had, that he'd fired you, that you'd told him you wouldn't let him have the machine. I didn't know he took the machine along with him."

"He fired you, didn't he, Ollie?"

"Yes. He came back and made up a lot of stuff about how I was stealing equipment."

Sherwood nodded. "He doesn't want you around to tell about the suppressor."

Ollie said, "He told me if I ever breathed a word about anything that happened in the center he'd get the FBI after me for a breach of security. That didn't scare me. But he also said if I ever returned to this country he'd get me sent to prison." He grinned. "That bothered me a little, but he didn't know about Gloria."

"Gloria Conners," Sherwood said.

"Yes. I went home for a while, just to go through the motions, you know, and then came back. Gloria and I are going to be married next week. I'm living at the Conners and staying out of sight."

Virginia, who had been quietly studying Ollie, said suddenly, "We're all forgetting one thing."

"What's that?" Sherwood asked.

"Dr. Schlessenger has made no apparent use of this suppressor-stimulator."

"Maybe he's biding his time. Or maybe he's sharpening his wits with it."

Virginia did not agree. "He'd have done something before this. In my book Dr. Schlessenger is a very vain man. He'd have done something."

"Maybe not, Virginia."

"And one other thing. Why didn't he erase Ollie's memory? That way it would have been complete and no one would have ever known. Surely he could have arranged that."

"I hadn't thought of that," Sherwood said. After a pause he said, "Well, there's only one way to find out and that's to see Dr. Schlessenger and ask him. Are you game, Ollie?"

"I guess so," Ollie said. "My only hope is he doesn't have the thing handy. I don't want to forget I'm engaged to a girl named Gloria."

CHAPTER SIXTEEN

DR. ANDREW SCHLESSENGER'S expression was that of outrage when Sherwood opened the door of his office without knocking and made Virginia and Ollie pass through before him. It was only when the doctor's eyes flickered over Ollie's face that they for a moment betrayed concern.

Miss Lawson, who had been bypassed in the maneuver, rushed in behind Sherwood, saying, "I didn't tell them they could come in, Doctor. They just walked by me..." She stood just inside the door, wringing her hands and looking for forgiveness in Schlessenger's face.

A woman sitting in the chair facing the doctor turned a face, pale and drawn, toward them. It was Mrs. Schlessenger. When her eyes met Sherwood's, she turned away.

Schlessenger said tersely, "You may leave, Miss Lawson," and his secretary backed out of the office, closing the door silently behind her after one sweeping, fearful look at the three persons standing on the thick carpet before the desk.

Then the doctor slid his cold blue eyes to Sherwood, and the two men studied each other for a long, decisive moment, a division of time that suddenly congealed into an opaque, impenetrable barrier which the doctor shattered by saying, "What do you expect to gain by this intrusion, Dr. Sherwood?"

Sherwood brought over a chair from the wall for Virginia, saying, "Our memories, Dr. Schlessenger."

"You won't find your memories in this office."

"Perhaps we can help you find yours, Doctor," Virginia said.

"I'm disappointed your husband has convinced you this is the right thing to do, Mrs. Sherwood. I've told you what to do about your mental lapse. I extended the services of qualified men to both of you."

"The trouble," Sherwood said quietly, "is not with us."

"Walter, if it weren't for the fact that you're sick—"

Sherwood smiled thinly. "Sick, Doctor?"

"Yes, sick. Your actions give every evidence of it, your delusions, your suspicions, your ideas that you're being persecuted. All are symptoms of a psychosis."

"Andrew—" Mrs. Schlessenger started to say.

"The pity of it is that we must all suffer." His glance rested briefly on her. "Including my wife." He turned back to Sherwood and demanded angrily, "Why for heaven's sake did you have to see her? You've upset her terribly."

"Maybe she had a reason to be upset," Sherwood said.

"Andrew," Mrs. Schlessenger said again, "I—"

"Georgia," Schlessenger said firmly, "I'm not going to let you become involved in this. Will you please go out to Miss Lawson's office until I finish in here."

"No, Andrew." She hunched down in her chair as if to become that much more unviewable, and Sherwood thought: She looks beaten, almost cringing and her face is the color of putty. What has Schlessenger done to her?

Schlessenger's face reddened in the wake of his wife's refusal to leave. He turned back to Sherwood and said, "You will have to go. I'm not going to allow Mrs. Schlessenger—"

"We'll leave," Virginia said scythe-like, "when you give us the suppressor-stimulator."

"The what?"

"The device Walter invented that erases memory."

Dr. Schlessenger's face could have exhibited no more surprise. "What kind of gibberish is that? What are you talking about?"

Sherwood said, "The machine I put in the safe when we went to California. You brought it along and used it at the motel."

Schlessenger slumped back in his chair, shook his head. "I'm willing to help you all I can, Walter, Mrs. Sherwood. I've told you both that. I offered to pay for treatment for either or both of you. I've offered to help you through school again. But coming in here talking nonsense doesn't help make me want to continue the offer. Where, for heaven's sake, did you latch on to this idea?"

Ollie said, "I told them."

The director's eyes, which had carefully avoided Ollie's, now came to rest on them. "You, Mr. Lansing, have no business in this office. I fired you and warned you what would happen if you ever returned. You are pressing me pretty far. I've had all the trouble I want out of you. You should apologize to these people for such a monstrous fabrication."

"Nobody," Virginia said, "expected you to come right out and admit anything, Doctor. You are saying only what we thought you would say."

Schlessenger shook his head. "I had always thought you had good judgment, Mrs. Sherwood. Obviously I credited you with more sense than you have." He sighed. "Or is it that you both so desperately want to be rid of your amnesia you will believe anything, even a tale told by an idiot?"

"It was no fabrication," Ollie said firmly.

Schlessenger looked him full in the face. "Maybe I'm wrong. Maybe you're not an idiot at all. Maybe you're cunning, trying to stir up the Sherwoods against me because I caught you pilfering laboratory equipment."

"It so happens," Sherwood said coldly, "that we believe Oliver Lansing."

"Believe him, then," Schlessenger snapped. "Make fools of yourselves if you want to. I don't know anything about a thing that suppresses memories. My God, I wish I did. The Institute could use a thing like that. If I had such a device would I be sitting here like this refuting it? I'd be shouting it from the rooftops I'd be having press conferences and Schlessenger Institute would be in all the papers!" He snorted. "All this is ridiculous."

"It is *not* ridiculous," Ollie said.

Schlessenger said cuttingly, "How would you know?"

"And that stuff about my stealing equipment is a lie!"

"Would you like me to name your fences in the Detroit University district?"

"Yes!" Ollie cried out hotly.

Sherwood said, "Let's not get off the track, Doctor. Ollie's not on trial here."

"I suppose you mean to imply that I am?"

"Yes."

"Then," Schlessenger said, "I'm afraid I will have to stop being civil and order you out of my office." He pushed a button on his desk and the answering buzz could be heard in the outer office.

Mrs. Schlessenger laid a white hand on her husband's arm. "Andrew, I want to say something."

At that moment Miss Lawson opened the door and Schlessenger said wearily, "Will you leave the door open, please? This meeting is over."

Sherwood took a step toward the massive desk. "This meeting is not over. In your laboratory behind that door I invented a device that was supposed to transmit images from one mind to another, only it didn't work out that way. It blanked out memory instead."

Schlessenger laughed. "That, my dear Dr. Sherwood, is a pipedream. A pipedream fresh from the imaginative head of your friend, Oliver Lansing. Now, if you please—"

Virginia said, "Your part in it fits very well, Doctor."

"Are you all going to get out of here," Schlessenger said, rising, his eyes slitted and menacing, "or am I going to have to throw you out?"

"Neither," Sherwood said. "You thought the suppressor-stimulator would stir your mind, make it sharper, perhaps raise your I.Q., so you worked out that trip to the West, just the three of us, real cozy, and when we reached Los Angeles you managed to get up enough nerve to blank out our minds, our memories for eleven years."

"Get out."

"A week's erasure for every half minute with the suppressor, Doctor. And afterwards you invented that story about my quitting."

"And," Ollie said, "you fired me and warned me to keep my mouth shut about it."

"You listen to me, Sonny," Schlessenger said angrily, "you're just damn lucky I didn't have you put in jail. It was only because such a scandal would involve the Institute that I—"

"Tell us, Doctor," Virginia said, "why you were so sympathetic to us, why you should offer treatment and schooling. That doesn't seem to go with your feelings about things. Could it be a compensation for what you did?"

"As of right this minute, those offers are null and void."

"Dr. Schlessenger," Sherwood said, "if you didn't take the device out of the safe, then it must still be there. Suppose you open the safe?"

"I'm opening no safe."

Sherwood withdrew a ring of keys from his pocket. "I'm sure one of these keys will fit the laboratory door. And there must be ways to open a safe." He started for the door to the laboratories.

"Stop where you are," Schlessenger said quietly. Sherwood stopped and turned at a new, ugly quality in Schlessenger's voice.

Schlessenger slid open a drawer, reached in and picked up a small, nickel-plated revolver, his eyes not leaving Sherwood's. "You are a trespasser, Dr. Sherwood, if you start to go through that door. As such I would be completely within my rights to kill you."

"Andrew," Mrs. Schlessenger said, rising between her husband and Sherwood, "this has gone far enough. I insist—"

Schlessenger moved to one side. "Sit down, Georgia," he said fiercely.

"I will not sit down, Andrew. I'm sick to death of all this. Did you hear that? Sick to death of it!"

"Georgia, this is no time—" Sherwood's movement toward the door caused him to move forward, forefinger tightening on the trigger. "Walter, I'm warning you!"

Sherwood ignored it, stepped toward the door.

"Andrew, you—!"

There was a sound of a struggle, the flash and boom of gunfire, but Sherwood felt nothing, halting, turning to the pall of smoke that billowed and eddied about the desk.

Mrs. Schlessenger, still alone near the desk, her face slack, her eyes staring at her husband, who was moving backward from her, the smoking gun in his hand, his eyes blinking, watching her as she collapsed, hitting the side of the desk and rolling off it to fall to the rug.

Then Schlessenger tottered on his feet, his face ashen, his eyes riveted to what lay on the floor, and he sent the hand with the gun to the desk to support himself.

When Sherwood moved toward Mrs. Schlessenger, the director jerked away from the desk, backing away, bringing the gun to bear on them all. His eyes were wild.

Miss Lawson, who had been standing all this time at the door, uttered a low moan, her eyes disappeared up into her head, and she slumped to the floor.

Schlessenger turned in her direction, stared for the briefest moment, then quickly crossed the floor, vaulted over the prostrate form through the door and was gone.

CHAPTER SEVENTEEN

THE SHOOTING OF Georgia Schlessenger, the realization by her husband of what he had done, and his resultant flight from the office, lightning fast as these things had been, seemed an incredible study in slow motion to the three people who observed them, rooting diem where they stood.

In a numb daze Sherwood heard the outer office door hiss closed, and his mind was suddenly flooded with a number of unrelated thoughts from which, like sluggish turtles emerging from the surf, came two demanding ones: Mrs. Schlessenger was in urgent need of attention, and he ought to stop the doctor. Even as he stood trying to decide which of these he should do he became aware of other faces, other voices, Rayburn's, Cox's, as they rushed in from the labs.

"See what you can do for Mrs. Schlessenger," he told Virginia as he grabbed Ollie's arm. "We've got to go after the doctor."

Then they stepped over the inert secretary, raced to the door and were outside in time to see the director's Cadillac spewing gravel as it spun around on the areaway and headed for the hard road.

As they ran for Sherwood's car and saw that Schlessenger was taking the road west, Sherwood knew it was a losing battle. The big car had more weight and speed. His own four-door was a fine car but simply lacked the power. Still, there was no alternative—or was there? He saw Mrs. Schlessenger's convertible there, gambled precious moments to see if she had left keys in it. When he saw she had, he jumped in, with Ollie crying, "Hey!" and Sherwood not answering but starting the car and sending it zooming out of its berth even before Ollie was settled, pressing him against the cushions, the door only half-closed.

When they reached the road, Schlessenger was not in sight. The highway was not a straight one, so it did not discourage Sherwood. He accelerated at full power, tires protesting as they whizzed around unbanked turns, until they came to a straightaway where they could see the other car. It was three blocks away.

It was then sheer power against power, the smooth motor of the convertible versus the equally good motor of the other car, and Sherwood didn't dare watch the speedometer, his right forearm pressed against the wheel so as not to lose control if a tire should suddenly blow. The surge of power was rewarded by an obvious lessening of distance.

"There's a bad curve up ahead," Ollie said, bracing himself and looking worriedly at Sherwood. "I know this road. He'll have to slow down."

"Okay," Sherwood said, reluctantly letting up on the accelerator. To his dismay the other car, now only a block ahead, crept away as it came to a small rise and sank quickly over it out of sight. Schlessenger wasn't slowing down.

When they reached the rise they were in a position to see more than a mile, the roadway before them dipping to a low point a few blocks distant. It was then that they saw the Schlessenger car barreling down the road with no compromise with danger, speedily heading for the curve in plain sight, the curve that ended in a clump of bushes and trees.

"He's a fool!" Ollie's voice jumped at him. "There's a bridge down there! He's not going to make it!"

They slowed and watched fascinatedly as the inevitable happened, just as if they were seeing it through a zoom lens that brought them closer. The other car started around the distant curve, teetering slightly on two wheels at first, slamming back on all four, then the other two, suddenly shaking in protest, doing a little dance, all at once flipping on its side, hitting an obstruction at the side of the road, catapulting into the air and end over end into the bushes and out of sight.

Sherwood braked the car at the curve's beginning, set the convertible well on the shoulder, and got out.

There wasn't a sound except the faint murmur of trickling water in a stream, a slight soughing of hot summer wind in the bushes, a bird's distant call. Something underfoot skittered away.

"He's dead," Ollie said as they ran across the road to the place where the bushes had been crushed by Schlessenger's big car.

"We don't know that."

"Nothing could have survived that."

They saw at the side of the road the train of logs that had accounted for the car's sudden jump end over end; one of the logs was split in two. They pressed their way through the thicket, broke into a low, clear area, saw the wreck a short distance away. It had come to rest on its wheels, oddly enough, a crumpled car with wrinkled fenders, a long gash along its top with jagged pieces of metal still holding splinters of wood, mud and grass and weeds. Through the broken, splintered windows they could see that Schlessenger hadn't been thrown out, and Sherwood thought it's a good thing because it's the throwing out that kills people and maybe he's still alive.

They reached the wreckage and Ollie grabbed a door handle. To his surprise the door came open with a shriek of metal-on-metal and sagged precariously on one hinge.

Schlessenger still sat in the driver's seat, his blond hair no longer neat and trim, his face flaccid, his blue eyes empty, staring, his expensive tweed suit torn, one foot twisted grotesquely to one side.

Sherwood thought at first he was dead—or unconscious. But he was neither, because the doctor, in a drunken twist of his head, suddenly knew they were there and tried to focus his eyes. He tried to move, clenched his teeth and moaned.

"Can you hear me?" Sherwood asked. "Can you understand me?"

Schlessenger mumbled something unintelligible and his head bobbed down, his chin resting on his chest, his forehead inches from the bent steering wheel.

Sherwood turned to Ollie, whose face was as white as Schlessenger's. "Think you could drive to town all right?"

Ollie stared at him.

Sherwood said, "Get hold of yourself. I want you to get an ambulance. I'll stay with him."

Ollie said, "I—" Then his eyes went wide and Sherwood turned to see Schlessenger sitting there looking at them, the revolver in his hand.

"No," Schlessenger said hoarsely, trying to control the nodding of his head. He drew lips away from his teeth and his breath whistled through them as he sought to bear his pain. His eyes became clearer and brighter with each passing moment.

Sherwood could see blood pulsing through a cut over his left eye, wondering oddly which way it would run, before he said, "I'm sending Ollie for an ambulance."

The gun muzzle came up in a tight fist. Schlessenger moved his shoulders a little and winced. The blood from the cut made a bright red rivulet down to his eyebrow. With his free hand he wiped the blood away. Again the clenched teeth and the word, "No."

"You can't sit there and bleed to death," Sherwood said. Schlessenger managed a crooked smile, motioned with the gun. "Stand closer together," he said in a whisper. "I want to get you both."

Sherwood made a move toward him, stopped when he saw the determination in the doctor's face.

"I had to kill one," Schlessenger said. "I didn't know it would be so easy." A tiny river of blood ran from the corner of his mouth. "Two more won't make any difference. Stand together. I haven't much time."

"Why?" Ollie said in a surprisingly calm voice. "Why must you kill us, Dr. Schlessenger?"

"Georgia will never tell. I'll never tell. Now you'll never tell."

"Tell what, Doctor?" Sherwood asked, his mind working furiously trying to find a way out of this.

Schlessenger's grin was evil. "You thought you won, didn't you, Walter. But you didn't. The door's been locked and the key's been thrown away."

They all listened as a car approached and passed.

Sherwood said desperately, "Dr. Schlessenger, you've had a bad accident and you need help. Your wife isn't dead, only hurt. You shouldn't talk. You should save your strength. You're going to need it."

Schlessenger gave a wry smile, the gun came up again, pointed straight at Sherwood. Now he grinned and said, "I'm the victor, Dr. Sherwood. I'm always the victor." Suddenly his head dipped a little and with effort he caught it and brought it up. His face was ashen and blood-streaked. He had difficulty in focusing his eyes.

Suddenly the hand with the gun jerked spasmodically, Schlessenger's eyes widened, his face twisted and he cried out, "Walter, damn you! Where are you? What are you doing to me?"

He gave a low moan as the life went out of his body, his face slackened, eyes glazed. His hand fell and the gun dropped to the floor from empty fingers and his limp body fell forward against the steering wheel.

CHAPTER EIGHTEEN

IF ANDREW SCHLESSENGER had died of natural causes there would not have been the repercussions and ramifications there were because of the manner of his going. Under ordinary circumstances the researchers could have weathered the flurry occasioned by his death, might have even continued their work without interruption, but the wounding of Mrs. Schlessenger and her husband's death in the car following the accident closed the Institute—"for a few days," authorities said—until the matter had been fully investigated.

The *Merrittville Record*, a weekly given to the goings and comings of the more prominent permanent residents, reports from area members in Congress, and releases from the Department of Agriculture, and which would have ordinarily given considerable space and prominence to the passing of such an important citizen as Dr. Schlessenger, did not disappoint its readers. The eulogy was there, but the shooting of his wife was relegated to a subordinate position, as if it were an afterthought, and all a mistake. Not so the Detroit, Grand Rapids and Lansing newspapers. They leaned heavily the other way, reading into the incident much more than the facts allowed, and since there was little else in the state news budget for the wire services, the story placed prominently news-wise.

There was no change in the townspeople—on the surface. They did not read the metropolitan papers more, nor did they read them less. They seemed to be indifferent to the several reporter and photographer teams that scurried about Merrittville and talked to everyone. But the townspeople did not ignore each other and, like Don Basilio's breath of detraction, the whispers grew until they far out-sized the already more-than-fair stretch of truth appearing in the daily papers.

Georgia Schlessenger, hospitalized with a shoulder wound (her condition was listed as "good"), told what she could to newsmen, the Merrittville police and sheriff's deputies (since her husband's death had taken place in the county), all of them reluctant but nonetheless willing to believe Dr. Schlessenger simply had gone berserk. She used the secret nature of Institute work as an excuse for not elaborating and telling why he so suddenly should have taken leave of his senses, merely implying overwork and the pressure of patronizing government agencies, which everybody seemed to understand.

One enterprising newspaperman who had sought out Dr. Schlessenger's secretary for an exclusive interview—with pictures—rushed to Mrs. Schlessenger's side, breathlessly demanding a confirmation or denial of certain fantastic angles of the story as divulged by Miss Lawson ("this business about a memory-a-suppressor, I think she said, and a stimulator, too") and his face colored a little with the telling.

Georgia Schlessenger merely laughed and told him if he wanted to she had no objection to his printing it ("But it is a little fantastic, wouldn't you say?") meanwhile making a note that Grace Lawson had just proved herself unfit to be anybody's secretary.

The newsman then asked if there was any truth to the rumor that one of the researchers and his wife suffered from amnesia, whereupon Mrs. Schlessenger asked him if he thought it likely that a man and wife would suffer amnesia at the same time, with or without the fantastic device referred to.

The reporter's face reddened even more, he coughed a little to cover his embarrassment and then, certain that Miss Lawson had gone off the deep end as a result of all that happened, he excused himself to pursue another line.

Sherwood was unprepared for the activity at 347 Walnut Street. First there were the rounds with the authorities and the newspapermen, and then there was Dr. Booey, who arrived and had to be brought up to date, to be followed by Virginia's parents, the Applebys, who had to be filled in too, and Sherwood was sure they never fully understood it. As if all this wasn't enough, the Coxes became frequent visitors, first for inside information and then to offer help. The upshot was that Sherwood had no time to think about any ultimate emergence from the cocoon of unremembrance—at least until Mrs. Schlessenger asked the Sherwoods to come to the hospital.

They saw a pale Georgia Schlessenger, her face nearly as white as the pillowcase, and when they first entered the sun-bright room, he thought: Even your freckles have faded, haven't they? Her eyes were larger and more liquid than he remembered them. They looked less troubled, too. Her hair tumbled in graceful waves over the pillow and she smiled when they came in, and the room, already bright, seemed to glow with it.

"I'm glad to see you," she said, raising her free right arm and offering her hand across the bed. "I've been sitting here thinking about you two. I would have sent for you" sooner but I just wasn't up to it. Besides, there were things I had to work out." She sat up, fluffed her pillow, slumped back and saw them still standing, so she said, "Sit down, sit down," and indicated two chairs at the bedside. "A not so young woman wants to say something."

"Don't talk that way," Virginia said, taking one of the chairs, "you're no old woman."

"I feel old," she said, sighing. "I feel at least two hundred years old." Then she smiled wryly. "But considering that I was shot at and hit, I'm feeling no great pain. Andrew was never a very good shot." A remembered incident clouded her eyes and her forehead wrinkled a little. Then she turned to Sherwood and said gravely, "But I won't say you and Mr. Lansing weren't in danger when you were standing beside the car. Let's just be thankful it ended the way it has."

Sherwood said, "I didn't mean to push Dr. Schlessenger into anything so violent."

"Don't excuse yourself," she said sharply. "You had every right to do what you did." Then she said with difficulty, haltingly, "I only wish it hadn't been necessary." Her eyes started to well with tears, but she fought them and looked out the hospital window to the rolling countryside of sand and bush and tree. "I warned Andrew, but he was one of those people who would never listen to anybody."

"You knew about it all," Sherwood said gently, "is that it?"

She turned back, saying, "Yes, I knew about it all, and I wanted to tell you, but I could never do it. I tried to make Andrew see it my way, but he never would. I was in the office pleading with him to let you know, trying to make him see how unfair it was, when you two came in with Oliver Lansing. I knew then it was the end—or the beginning." She smiled bleakly and went on, "As it turned out, it was both."

After a moment, Virginia said, "Both?"

Mrs. Schlessenger said, "I will explain, but I'd better go back to the beginning." She looked out the window again as if to search there for a place to start. "Andrew was an opportunist. I knew that when I married him. I thought our association together would blossom into something beautiful in spite of the fact that I felt from the start that he didn't love me. My mistake was thinking I could ever change him. But I learned nobody ever changed Andrew. The tragedy is that I had to learn so late.

"I didn't know at first he was such a liar and cheat. For years I kept him surrounded by an aura that existed only in my mind. It was like wearing glasses that don't focus right—or being without glasses when you need them. What I'm trying to say is that I never saw Andrew clearly for years. He was blurred. It was much later that my vision cleared and I found him to be the man you know he was. You'd be surprised at the things I discovered about him—things that made me wonder if he even had any right to his degrees. But don't misunderstand me, there was nothing stupid about Andrew in spite of the things he claimed that were not true. He was, in his way, a rather brilliant man, a man always putting himself to the test, compounding his lies and being successful in covering one group with another. It was a pity he used his intelligence for such a petty thing. He wasted his life covering up his deceits. He never seemed to realize he could have gone just as far being an honest man."

For several minutes she was lost in her thoughts, lips parted slightly, looking out to the distant sand hills. Then she said, "Perhaps it was a mistake to suggest the Institute. I thought if he had real responsibilities—in this case to the government, the National Science Foundation, the employees, Merrittville itself, and to me—he might change and become the man I knew he could be if he wanted.

"For a long time I thought it was working. Andrew was happy at the Institute and the knowledge that he was the director of it gave him a real-life position of respect. He made several unfortunate choices in researchers, was angry when the National Science Foundation did not see eye-to-eye with him about procedure and program. I think he was actually surprised when they said they expected results. I think he suddenly realized the Institute was no playhouse, that he would have to produce. He knew he couldn't count on the friends he had hired, so he put out hooks for promising young researchers, found you and Mr. Cox, and because he wanted to show the National Science Foundation they didn't know what they were talking about, he kept after you two to produce something truly sensational."

Georgia Schlessenger fluffed the pillow again. "I first heard of the TV idea about a year ago. Andrew said you were working on a device to shoot thoughts into people's heads. He didn't talk much about it because he didn't think it could be done, but one night he came home all disturbed. You'd told him you'd given the machine a try and erased memory instead that got him started along a new line and he thought of any number of uses for such a thing, all with mounting enthusiasm; some of his ideas make me ashamed to remember them, but that was another thing about Andrew: He had no shame. Sometimes I think he told me things just to taunt me. He thought I was too stiff and unbending because I refused to descend to his level.

"He became really excited later when you told him how you thought the machine could raise intelligence levels and aid memory through temporary lapse. He told me he noticed the change in you and the way he talked I knew he envied it. He tried to get you to let him try it, but you said it wasn't perfected yet."

Mrs. Schlessenger smiled. "He was like a small boy. When you told him he'd have to wait, he stamped his foot and told you he was director of the Institute and he was ordering you to let him use it. You just shrugged and told him there was plenty of time, that you had to iron out a few of the bugs before you'd trust anybody else with it. At least that's what Andrew said when he came home storming about it, and I guess it was true. I never saw him quite so furious." She managed a little laugh. "One moment Dr. Sherwood was a wonderful man, a man full of ideas and promise, the researcher who was going to save the Institute and make the men at the National Science Foundation sit up and take notice. The next moment you were a man to be watched because you were going to keep your little device all to yourself. You were no longer to be trusted and you were trying to cheat the Institute out of what was rightfully Andrew's. That shows how he rationalized everything."

"Without a memory, a man needs not be watched," Sherwood said. "So he erased ours."

"It wasn't impulsive. It was a thing that grew, much as a malignant thing does, little by little, until it can't be rooted out. First he worked on you in the laboratory, tried to bring you around to share the suppressor-stimulator with him. But I don't think you trusted him any more when you saw how anxious he was. I think you were afraid he'd misuse it or perhaps announce it was his own discovery. Oh, I don't know just what you did think, but I do know you didn't leave it in the lab. You took it home with you every night. Poor, frustrated Andrew! How he kept wishing you'd forget it just once!

"Then when he saw he wasn't going to get the device itself, he started his plans jag, which is what I finally called it. He was after you night and day to draw plans for the device. 'Suppose something happened to you, Walter?' he'd say. 'Where would the Institute be?' But you said the Institute would still have the machine. Then he'd say, 'But suppose something happened to you and the machine?' Then, I remember Andrew telling it—and he didn't think it was funny—you said, 'Well, suppose I draw the plans and something happens to me and the machine and the plans? Aren't plans just something else to worry about?'

"That only made Andrew more angry, more furtive. You were sidestepping every thrust. It never occurred to Andrew that he could have gained everything by simply being straightforward; your resistance only made him more compulsive than ever about it. The machine, he'd have to get the machine. The machine, all the time, the machine. He didn't really think about what he'd do with it when he got it; his whole life settled into scheming to get it."

Mrs. Schlessenger stopped, her right hand picking at the bedspread. "It became so important that he get it that Andrew ate little and slept less. For the machine he was ready to go farther than he had ever gone for anything in his life. He was, in fact, ready to kill for it."

Her eyes came up challengingly. "I shouldn't say that, perhaps, but it is true. I can only thank God that he didn't carry out some of the plans he had. The thing he did do is bad enough. When he left with you for California I knew it wasn't what it appeared to be—a simple trip to the convention—and I confronted Andrew with it, challenged him, told him I knew he was going to do something. We had a scene before he left, but he refused to say anything. I think he was afraid I would somehow be able to warn you, knowing how I felt about the way he was thinking."

There was a pause and Sherwood said, "When he came back from California he told you I had quit, I suppose?"

"No," Mrs. Schlessenger said, frowning, lost in the remembered return of her husband. "Not right away. I heard it from someone else—I think it was from Mrs. Cox." Remembering the return more vividly now, she narrowed her eyes a little. "No, Andrew didn't tell me anything about you. He was far too upset for that."

Virginia said, "Upset, Mrs. Schlessenger?"

"Yes. I suppose you know how he managed to get the machine?"

"I had to put it somewhere," Sherwood said. "I guessed he got it out of the safe. Is that right?"

"Yes. He went to the office an hour before you started west. He was very jubilant that morning. You know, too, how the erasure was handled?"

"The head of our bed was next to his wall. He put the device on a chair or something on his side and let it run most of the night."

"That's right. Andrew thought he was particularly clever doing that."

Virginia reminded her, "You said Dr. Schlessenger was upset when he returned."

"He was. You see, the morning after he erased your memories he picked up the machine in its leather box, rented a car to go to Santa Barbara for the convention. On the way he had an accident. A sports car sideswiped his car, crushed the suitcase containing the suppressor-stimulator. Neither Andrew nor the other driver was hurt, but the gadget was wrecked. Andrew said he cried like a baby when he picked up the pieces. He could hardly keep from weeping when he was telling me about it."

"So the machine is ruined," Sherwood said gravely.

"Yes, the machine is ruined," Mrs. Schlessenger said. "Andrew brought it back, tried to work it over, but it was beyond repair and he had no idea what went where—or even if it was all there."

Sherwood sighed wearily, left the chair and went to the window Mrs. Schlessenger had been looking out of. "That's what Dr. Schlessenger meant when he said the door's been locked and the key's been thrown away."

"He said that?"

"Yes. He also said he was the final victor. I guess he's right." He turned to her. "Where is the gadget now? In the safe?"

"Yes. That's why he didn't want you to go back to the lab."

"I'd like to take a look at it."

Virginia said brightly, "I see now why Dr. Schlessenger couldn't erase Ollie's memory. I'll wager he'd planned to do it when he returned and was pretty hard put to think of a way to get rid of him."

Sherwood grunted. "No wonder he didn't do anything with the outfit. He didn't even have it, or at least he didn't have a working model of it. And as a result all he needed to do was sit tight and hope Ollie never showed up, hope you would never say anything. Who could prove anything? What law covers deliberate erasure of memory?"

Mrs. Schlessenger said, "He was determined to have his toy at any price, except that when he did get it, it was ruined for him. Still he thought he'd be able to talk and think his way out of this bigger lie, the biggest one, he'd ever lived. It was too bad he didn't have the device to improve his memory and raise his intelligence. He might have become the—who can say what he would have done? I've thought of it often enough."

Sherwood said dismally, "But since it's broken and there's no way to put it back together—"

"Not necessarily, Dr. Sherwood. Andrew was certain you made some sort of schematic, some sort of diagram. He mentioned that to me several times."

"It may have been wishful thinking."

"No. He said he saw you working on a diagram, that's how sure he was."

Mrs. Schlessenger's voice had changed a little and Sherwood looked at her sharply. There was a brightness of eye, a flush of cheek, and he was puzzled by it. He said, "How sure are you that such a thing exists?"

She answered his look with steady eyes. "Sure enough to offer you something."

"What?"

"The Institute. I want you to run it the way it ought to be run."

Virginia said in surprise, "You want Walter to run the Institute? Why, Mrs. Schlessenger?"

"Why?" Her eyes flickered to her coolly, then they warmed and she smiled, saying, "I will be frank with you, Mrs. Sherwood. I think Walter was made for the Institute. Oh, not the Walter we see before us now, but the Walter that was. He was much more the director than Andrew ever was. He is what I wanted Andrew to be, and I want him to have the Institute very much, Mrs. Sherwood."

Seeing the uncertain look in Virginia's eyes, she went on tightly, "As for myself, I've had enough of Merrittville. I think I shall go to Europe, someplace in Europe."

CHAPTER NINETEEN

IN their missing state the plans were as much of an obstacle as Schlessenger had ever been, and when they were not quickly found, they focused on the possibility of reassembling the suppressor-stimulator, a disarray of wires, crumpled printed circuits, transistors and crystals.

Booey grunted when he saw it. "This is more confusing than not finding it at all," he said, rubbing his bald head with the flat of his hand. "I thought I had a pretty good idea of what it would look like, but it was nothing like this." He shook his head and pushed around a few of the pieces on the lab desk.

Ollie was helpful, but while he knew where most of the components went, he could not explain how they were hooked up. "Besides," he said, "I don't recall half of this stuff. I think Schlessenger mixed something else with this."

That's when the work turned in earnest to the missing diagram, the reality of which Ollie could vouch for. Did you actually see them? he was asked. No, he said. Could they have existed? Yes. What would they look like? Probably ink on tough paper. Would they have been made in the laboratory? Probably.

It always came back to that. The schematics would have to be in the lab. Were they still there?

They spent many hours searching, looking behind drawers, on the underside of drawers, tapping the woodwork on desks and on the wall and molding. When they were sure the diagrams could not possibly be in the laboratory, they moved to Schlessenger's desk and file, just in case he had found them and had not been able to make use of them yet. Then they moved to the other rooms and the other laboratories, always with the same result.

Finally, certain there was no chance the diagrams could be at the Institute, they moved out of the building, Sherwood, Ollie, Booey and Appleby, deciding to do Sherwood's house next. They went over it inch-by-inch, tapping boards again for secret places and panels. But it was fruitless, and when it was over the exhausted searchers could think of nowhere else to look.

Appleby said at last, "I think we'd all feel better if we went fishing," and when Booey laughed because the idea was the farthest thing from his mind, Appleby went on, "No, I mean it—they're biting good everywhere. And I mean the big fish. Deep-sea fishing in the Bay."

"That would be giving up," Sherwood said. "I for one couldn't fish thinking about those plans."

"If I had a cow that I couldn't find," Appleby said, "I'd do something else for a while and in the meantime try to figure out where I'd have gone if I were a cow."

Booey laughed at this. "I think you're right. We're trying too hard. What do you say, Walter?"

"No, Doctor. You fellows go ahead."

Ollie said hopefully, "I've never been deep-sea fishing." When they were gone, Sherwood wished that he had gone with them, thinking how ridiculous it was for him to stay behind when he could have thought just as well out on the water. He went upstairs and lay on the bed, trying to relax every muscle so he could give his entire body over to the problem of what the insulated part of his mind had done with the drawings. They must be somewhere, he told himself. Think, think, think! And all he could conjure before his mind's eye were fish, jumping out of the water.

Next he tried putting himself in his place, as Appleby had done with his cows, but he got nowhere doing this.

"You should have gone fishing," Virginia said when she came upstairs to find out why he was so quiet.

"I know it."

"Why didn't you go?

"I thought thinking about the diagrams was more important."

"You could have thought—"

"I know. I could have thought about them while I was fishing. I thought of that. But too late." He sat up so that they were side by side on the bed. "But really I shouldn't really have gone. Do you realize we're nearly there? Within inches. Only one more mystery to solve and we'll remember everything."

She did not look at him but watched the trees beyond the window stirred by vagrant breezes. "I wish you'd forget about those plans for a while."

"I'll forget about them when we find them, when we build another gadget and reverse what's happened."

"Is it so important to you, Walter?"

He looked at her sharply. "Are you telling me again it's not important to you?"

"There are other things," she said tonelessly, still not trusting herself to look at him.

"Such as?"

She swung around to face him. "We have to live, don't we? We don't stop breathing because we don't have those plans of yours, do we?"

"Sometimes," he said in a strangled voice, "I don't think you really want to find them."

"I know what you think," she said quietly. "I know. But until we do I think we should try to live like normal people. If we never find them we may have to live that way anyway."

When Sherwood said nothing she went on, "I'm going down to the bank and find out how much money we have and if there isn't much in the account I'm going to look for a job. I like Merrittville. I like this house. I think we ought to stay here with or without the plans." She rose so suddenly he was jounced on the bed. She walked from the room.

Later Mrs. Appleby looked in on him. "You're young," she said. "Don't take it so hard. After all, what's a day or two?"

He was about to say something to her when she said, "You should have gone fishing, you know," and was gone. He thought: Everyone thinks I should have gone fishing maybe they're right maybe I am taking it too hard. Are eleven years so damned important after all?"

The fishing was over, the trout, baked over a charcoal fire in the back yard, were delicious, and everyone was sitting around in the living room and Sherwood was thinking the fishing and the eating isn't all that's over. I can feel it, almost stumble over it here in this house.

Booey was talking about his work back at Chicago, Ollie had suddenly become impatient with everything and had been called to the phone twice because Gloria Conners was becoming impatient too, and Homer Appleby was talking about the weather "up here in the little finger of Michigan" although it wasn't quite the little finger, and Mrs. Appleby was telling the Coxes, who had come over, just how she made cherry pie back in Illinois. Through it all Virginia was sitting glum-faced and Sherwood thought my, her face is pale and strained I wonder what's wrong with her she's been acting strangely tonight.

"It shouldn't be too hard," Booey was saying.

"What?"

"I say, it shouldn't be too hard duplicating the machine."

"Sure," Sherwood said, seeing Virginia's round eyes on his. He rose to go over to talk with her, but Ollie interrupted by saying, "I suppose I ought to be shoving off, Doctor. I told Gloria I'd be coming over."

"Everybody talking about leaving," Appleby said, "reminds me we've got to go back in the morning. Can't be away from a farm too long, you know. Like having a babysitter; you never quite trust a stranger."

Cox said, "What do you think you'll do, Walt?"

Sherwood turned to him and thought that is The Question, isn't it? What do I do now that I can't find the key? He said, "Frankly, I don't know, Hamp."

"Maybe you ought to try school," Mrs. Appleby said cheerfully. "It's not such a bad idea."

"I don't think so, Mrs. Appleby," Sherwood said emptily, weary of thinking about it. He found Virginia's eyes again and was startled to see how white her face had become. As he looked at her she stood up and he thought for a moment she was going to cry, but she turned, left the room, walked through the hallway to the kitchen.

No one said anything. They all heard the door close. Booey turned to him and said, "You'd better go to her, Walt," but Sherwood was already halfway across the room.

He found Virginia, a dark, solitary figure on the bench beneath the back yard beech tree. She did not move when he sat next to her. She was looking at the moon but not seeing it.

After a while he said, "What's the matter?"

When she did not answer he said, "I thought you were quite happy the way things are. I just don't understand this."

She closed her eyes and he was more puzzled than ever. She compressed her lips, held her eyes tightly closed.

"Virginia…"

She released her breath, reached for his hand. "I'm sorry. I'm just afraid, that's all."

"Afraid?"

"Afraid things will change too much." She brushed a lock of hair out of her eyes. "Things have been fine with us these few days."

"Things needn't change." He reached for her chin, brought her head around so he could look directly into her eyes. "Things will always be fine with us. There's no need to think otherwise."

"Kitty has told me how you used to be."

"How did I used to be?"

"Seldom home. A walking computer and slide rule and book of formulas. You buried yourself out at the Institute and seldom came up for air. Most of the time I rattled around in the house all by myself."

He said levelly, "It won't be like that."

The back door slammed and they turned to see Booey coming toward them. "I'm intruding, I hope," he said.

"I've been hearing about what a heel I was." Booey grunted. "The typical dedicated man who holes himself up in a laboratory with an eye for knurled knobs. That's what you were like at Ryerson." He hunted around, found a lawn chair, dragged it over to them, saying, "I suppose you were just like that at the Institute."

"A recluse."

"You won't need to stay that way. After all, you will have all that's happened recently to remember. That should get you out of the laboratory more often." He added soberly, "I wanted to talk with you both. I wanted to say that neither of you should sit in judgment on the unremembered part. You're incomplete persons, both of you."

"And," Sherwood said bitterly, "we're apt to remain that way."

"Think so? I don't. I know what you're both thinking. Given the chance, should you go back? Walter, I honestly believe Virginia could convince you to give up the idea, which is good because it is a wonderful thing to think so much of someone you would be willing to forego what once was. And you, Virginia, you're hardly the perky girl with spirit who had enough energy left over after solving her own problems to help others with theirs. Have you forgotten how to fight? Have you forgotten how you fought to get off the farm because you had a larger vision? Have you both forgotten how you fought your way this far out of an eleven years' blindness?"

"Doctor," Sherwood said.

"Virginia," Booey went on, "you will still have a fight on your hands. You will have had a breather. Now you can go in and compete with Walter's fascinating mistress—science. Do you have any fight left?"

"You're forgetting," Sherwood said, "that we don't have that choice to make."

Somewhere a cicada sang loud and long and Booey waited until it was through to say, "Something else. Droughts and seasons register on the trees and what we are is the result of our experiences, whether we're a leaf on that tree or a human being on God's green earth. What you say to each other here in your back yard tonight will be as much a part of you as that part that you will suddenly remember when you're stimulated to remember it all again. Remembering it, you will know how you feel now and you'll have to compromise with your old personalities. I'm sure it will be a change for the better. In fact, you two people have had an opportunity denied most people. You've seen yourselves really objectively."

Virginia stood up, walked around Booey, stood looking toward the darkness of the bushes and trees.

"Lastly," Booey said, dropping his voice and looking away, "every last human being on this earth is a repository for others. We live in other people. And when one of our friends die, then that part of us that has lived in him dies, too. By refusing to embrace that part of friends that is hidden in the unremembered part of you, you're killing that part of them that is in you. I'm sure you wouldn't want to do that. It would be very unkind. Wouldn't it, Virginia?"

She turned, tears glistening in her eyes. "Yes, it would be most unkind, Doctor." Suddenly she broke away and started running for the house.

Sherwood stood up, ready to pursue her.

"Stay," Booey said. "Let her go."

"What is wrong with her?" Sherwood asked, and when Booey said nothing, he went on, "What was all that about? I didn't understand you."

"It's not Dr. Booey you don't understand," Booey said. "It's Virginia."

"Why?"

Booey turned a grave face to his. "She found the diagrams. They were in the safety deposit box at the bank. She opened it this afternoon and saw them there. Right now they're upstairs in her dresser underneath her lingerie where I told her to put them until she made up her mind to tell you about them." He turned his head, looked up at the house to the second floor room now flooded with light. He chuckled, "I fancy she will be down with them in a few moments. Then we shall go to work."

THE END

If you've enjoyed this book, you will not want to miss these terrific titles...

ARMCHAIR SCI-FI, FANTASY, & HORROR DOUBLE NOVELS, $12.95 each

D-1 **THE GALAXY RAIDERS** by William P. McGivern
SPACE STATION #1 by Frank Belknap Long

D-2 **THE PROGRAMMED PEOPLE** by Jack Sharkey
SLAVES OF THE CRYSTAL BRAIN by William Carter Sawtelle

D-3 **YOU'RE ALL ALONE** by Fritz Leiber
THE LIQUID MAN by Bernard C. Gilford

D-4 **CITADEL OF THE STAR LORDS** by Edmund Hamilton
VOYAGE TO ETERNITY by Milton Lesser

D-5 **IRON MEN OF VENUS** by Don Wilcox
THE MAN WITH ABSOLUTE MOTION by Noel Loomis

D-6 **WHO SOWS THE WIND...** by Rog Phillips
THE PUZZLE PLANET by Robert A. W. Lowndes

D-7 **PLANET OF DREAD** by Murray Leinster
TWICE UPON A TIME by Charles L. Fontenay

D-8 **THE TERROR OUT OF SPACE** by Dwight V. Swain
QUEST OF THE GOLDEN APE by Ivar Jorgensen and Adam Chase

D-9 **SECRET OF MARRACOTT DEEP** by Henry Slesar
PAWN OF THE BLACK FLEET by Mark Clifton.

D-10 **BEYOND THE RINGS OF SATURN** by Robert Moore Williams
A MAN OBSESSED by Alan F. Nourse

ARMCHAIR SCIENCE FICTION CLASSICS, $12.95 each

C-1 **THE GREEN MAN**
by Harold M. Sherman

C-2 **A TRACE OF MEMORY**
By Keith Laumer

ARMCHAIR MASTERS OF SCIENCE FICTION SERIES, $16.95 each

M-1 **MASTERS OF SCIENCE FICTION, Vol. One**
Bryce Walton—"Dark of the Moon" and other tales

M-2 **MASTERS OF SCIENCE FICTION, Vol. Two**
Jerome Bixby: "One Way Street" and other tales

If you've enjoyed this book, you will not want to miss these terrific titles…

ARMCHAIR SCI-FI & HORROR DOUBLE NOVELS, $12.95 each

D-11   **PERIL OF THE STARMEN** by Kris Neville
            THE STRANGE INVASION by Murray Leinster

D-12   **THE STAR LORD** by Boyd Ellanby
            CAPTIVES OF THE FLAME by Samuel R. Delaney

D-13   **MEN OF THE MORNING STAR** by Edmund Hamilton
            PLANET FOR PLUNDER by Hal Clement and Sam Merwin, Jr.

D-14   **ICE CITY OF THE GORGON** by Chester S. Geier and Richard S. Shaver
            WHEN THE WORLD TOTTERED by Lester Del Rey

D-15   **WORLDS WITHOUT END** by Clifford D. Simak
            THE LAVENDER VINE OF DEATH by Don Wilcox

D-16   **SHADOW ON THE MOON** by Joe Gibson
            ARMAGEDDON EARTH by Geoff St. Reynard

D-17   **THE GIRL WHO LOVED DEATH** by Paul W. Fairman
            SLAVE PLANET by Laurence M. Janifer

D-18   **SECOND CHANCE** by J. F. Bone
            MISSION TO A DISTANT STAR by Frank Belknap Long

D-19   **THE SYNDIC** by C. M. Kornbluth
            FLIGHT TO FOREVER by Poul Anderson

D-20   **SOMEWHERE I'LL FIND YOU** by Milton Lesser
            THE TIME ARMADA by Fox B. Holden

ARMCHAIR SCIENCE FICTION CLASSICS, $12.95 each

C-3   **INTO PLUTONIAN DEPTHS**
           by Stanton A. Coblentz

C-4   **CORPUS EARTHLING**
           by Louis Charbonneau

C-5   **THE TIME DISSOLVER**
           by Jerry Sohl

C-6   **WEST OF THE SUN**
           by Edgar Pangborn

ARMCHAIR SCIENCE FICTION & HORROR GEMS SERIES, $12.95 each

G-1   **SCIENCE FICTION GEMS, Vol. One**
           Isaac Asimov and others

G-2   **HORROR GEMS, Vol. One**
           Carl Jacobi and others